Happy Days

Jenny Worstall

Copyright © 2021 Jenny Worstall

All rights reserved

The characters and events portrayed in this book are fictitious. Any similarity to real persons, living or dead, is coincidental and not intended by the author.

No part of this book may be reproduced, or stored in a retrieval system, or transmitted in any form or by any means, electronic, mechanical, photocopying, recording, or otherwise, without express written permission of the publisher.

For boarding survivors everywhere

Contents

Title Page

Copyright

Dedication

Chapter 1	1
Chapter 2	8
Chapter 3	16
Chapter 4	27
Chapter 5	36
Chapter 6	49
Chapter 7	56
Chapter 8	66
Chapter 9	75
Chapter 10	84
Chapter 11	95
Chapter 12	104
Chapter 13	113

Chapter 14	118
Chapter 15	126
Chapter 16	135
Chapter 17	141
Chapter 18	148
Chapter 19	154
Chapter 20	160
Chapter 21	166
About The Author	175

Chapter 1

First night at boarding school

I stood by an open door peering into the dark night sky studded with stars, feeling a cool breeze on my raw cheeks. The sharp metal slats of the boot mat pressed into my feet through my thin cotton slippers. I sniffed the earthy autumn air and thought of home, wanting to cry but with no tears left. How had this happened? How could I be standing here clad in my night clothes in an alien world, a World of Women, chilly and bereft?

It had all started five weeks ago, at the end of July 1970, when my parents had told me I would not be returning to my day school in September as they would be moving to Italy. We visited a large rambling country mansion in Dorset, 'to see if you like the look of the school'. My father parked outside the gothic front door and I was allowed to grasp the metal bell pull and yank it until a faint tinkling could be heard.

"Are all the adults here women?" I asked my mother.

She nodded, her eyes glinting.

"And will this be my school until I am grown up?"

"Yes," my father said. "You will attend St Hilda's Convent School every term until you are a woman too."

And so here I was, on my way back to bed after visiting the bathroom on the first night at my new school, taking the opportunity to stand by an open door and gulp mouthfuls of fresh night air. I took a hesitant step forward, then another, until I was outside the building looking across the cobbled courtyard, my blood racing as I considered possibilities.

I knew the way under the arch to the left and round the side of the school to the mile-long drive; the moon was out, I liked walking and was sure I'd soon warm up. Once I reached the wide gate at the end, I'd go...which way? I closed my eyes. Which way had the car turned into the school drive this morning? Right? No, surely the left, because if I had been sitting on the left, my usual side, then I would have seen...oh, it was no use. I couldn't picture it. Perhaps if I went down the drive to the main road, I might be able to remember.

Hearing a sudden sound, I looked up. I was in the middle of the courtyard now. A figure appeared at the window opposite as a light was snapped on and I could see an older girl in her study bedroom briefly before she pulled the curtains. That was close! I crept to the side of the courtyard, my breath rasping. Stretching my back to try to breathe more comfortably, I hoped my crackling old friend asthma wouldn't get the better of me.

I could continue with my great escape, but perhaps I should be sensible. Did I really think it was a good idea to try to make my way back home to my parents, under my own steam, in the dark? With no transport arranged, without knowing which road to take, and dressed in my night clothes? Besides, they might already be travelling to the airport, making their way to a new life, to sunshine.

A dark shape swooped over me and I shrank against the rough wall, jagged stones pulling at my dressing gown. A girl on my table at supper this evening had told me she'd seen bats dive bombing the school at night.

I thought back to when we had unpacked our trunks this afternoon, kneeling on the fragrant polished floorboards of the vast panelled Hall; we heaped our possessions into blankets before dragging them along dim corridors to the Cubicles. Books were inspected by Sister Edward and those she considered suitable were lightly pencilled with her initials, but any that were deemed either worthless or too advanced were confiscated until the end of term.

I argued a bit about my treasured copy of *The Diary of Anne Frank*; it obviously wasn't worthless, so what was wrong with it?

"It is not suitable because it will scare and upset

you. Poor Anne and her family were virtual prisoners in the tiny attic until, well, until things got far worse. Do not question me further. You are not to read it."

"But Sister Edward, it's one of my favourite books."

"You mean you've read it? Your parents let you read it?" Sister Edward's eyebrows shot up until they nearly disappeared under her wimple.

"Yes! I love it! I brought it with me because I want to read it again."

Sister Edward had adjusted her cape and smoothed down the gathered folds of her floor length habit.

"You can have it back at the end of term and read it again in the holidays, if that is the sort of thing your parents let you do. While you are here, you will read what I decide."

A desolate sorrow for the loss of my beloved book swept over me and I curled my fingers into balls of rage. I couldn't stay here, where others decided what I read. I had to leave and it had to be now.

Steadying my breathing, I walked under the arch of the Clock Tower, and past the Refectory where we had eaten fried bread, cauliflower cheese and gristly sausages this evening. The rows of beech trees lining the winding pot-holed drive rustled and beckoned me into their gentle embrace. Should I? Dare I? I put my leg out to take a step and waited. If I allowed my foot to touch the ground pointing towards the drive, the road to freedom, the decision was made – I was off and never coming back. I didn't care what any of the adults might say and I knew they'd all say plenty: I didn't belong here and that was that.

If my parents had already left, I'd make my way to my aunt in Devon; she'd look after me – she'd understand. She might even allow me to live with her and attend a day school.

My leg hovered above the ground, shin aching as if on fire. The shrubbery in the far distance shivered and I could see, what was it? A black shape – a shadowy figure? A veil?

I hopped round, managing to prevent my foot from touching the ground, then raced back to the Cubicles, heart pounding, as I knew all along I would. I was going back to the safety of my prison, to my lino-floored cubicle with its tiny pink basin, narrow bed, and thin curtain separating me from all the other sleeping girls in their cells. I was such a coward.

I told myself I'd do it one day, but not now, not tonight. You had to plan if you wanted to run away and change your life and I wasn't ready; I wasn't wearing the right clothes and had no money for the journey – and what if there actually had been something or someone watching me from the shrubbery? Running away was a ridiculous idea. Childish in the extreme.

I slid into bed quickly and pulled the covers over me, still wearing my dressing gown. Early September and it was freezing.

Snuggling down, I considered the possibility that I might have missed my only chance to escape. I should have been bold and got away before it was too late, because if you wait until you're completely ready and prepared to leave, if you put it off again and again, everything will seem different; you'll have given your life away and forgotten what it was you wanted to do and who you wanted to be.

Suddenly, a veiled head popped through the curtain and a pair of beady eyes peered into my soul. It was Sister Edward.

"Still awake? This won't do."

I sat up and asked if I could have my light on to read.

"It's too late. Lie down. There, there."

Sister Edward stroked my head gently but uncertainly, causing the tears I had thought were finished to spout forth again.

"You're homesick; it will pass. Sleep now."

As she glided away, I turned onto my side and a comforting thought occurred; maybe it wouldn't be quite as bad here as I had thought? Maybe if I tried really hard, I'd manage to hold onto who I was and hold onto my dreams of who I wanted to become – despite the lengthy sentence I would have to endure imprisoned in the World of Women.

As I drifted towards sleep, a black shape rustled into my cubicle and placed something on the chair next to my bed; a veil swished away and I twisted to investigate. My copy of *The Diary of Anne Frank* had been restored to me! I picked it up and placed it under my pillow.

Maybe six years wouldn't be such a long time after all.

Chapter 2

A glimmer of hope

Early the next morning, my curtain was whisked back by a cheery sixth former, her heels clattering on the hard floor.

"Wake up! Benedicamus Domine!"

This was so different from my mother's gentle voice asking if I'd had a good night, or my father's jolly shout of 'Show a leg!', that I felt bewildered and struggled to remember where I was.

Then it hit me like a sledgehammer. St Hilda's Convent School. Here I was, until the end of term. Twelve long weeks before I could go home...but it wouldn't be home, would it? Because my parents had moved to Rome. Another new place to get used to.

Tears of self-pity started up again and the curtain twitched on my left.

"Cry baby! Hey, everyone – New Bug's crying again!"

Natalie, a thin wiry girl with currant eyes and a sneering expression was peering at me. She inhabited the next door cubicle – she'd been at the school since she was seven and knew everyone and everything.

"Stop that!" the sixth former said sternly, wagging her finger at Natalie. "Crikey though, New Bug, oops, sorry, I mean Trixie, you'd better get a move on, spit spot, the line's already forming and here you are still in bed."

Muffled giggles from around the Cubicles told me what my fellow prisoners thought of me, causing the sixth former to grab my uniform from the chair at the side of my bed and whisper,

"Come on! It's not that bad! Pop this on – no time to wash today – and if I were you, I'd act like you don't care. These idiots who are teasing you, it's only for a laugh. They'll be your best friends by the end of the week – just you wait and see."

I got dressed faster than I had ever done in my life and shrank into the line that was forming like a writhing snake down the length of the Cubicles.

"Quiet!" Sister Edward bellowed. "I will not have shouting! It is so unladylike."

I trembled and shuffled forwards as we made our way, heads bowed, along the beeswax-filled corridors to the Chapel entrance. My place was at the end of the queue as my surname was at the bottom of the alphabet, but I was grateful for this as it meant no one could stare at me.

"Eyes forward!" Sister Edward screamed. "No chatting! Say a silent prayer as you enter the holy building – ask for God's forgiveness."

I entreated God to forgive me for all the things I had ever done wrong that could possibly have resulted in my being sent here.

We were ushered into the wide honey-coloured pine benches and instantly had to kneel on thin hard vinyl cushions, especially uncomfortable for those who, like me, were bony in the knee department. I closed my eyes and clasped my hands in front of me, sending a silent prayer to the heavens.

Please God, let St Hilda's not be too bad – please?

A bell rang for the beginning of Mass and Father Cuthbert limped up a flight of wide shallow carpeted steps to the altar, dressed in brightly embroidered robes, his black trousers poking out from underneath. There was a strong smell of something I couldn't quite place and I wrinkled my nose.

"War wound," my neighbour whispered helpfully. "I'm Cath, by the way. I'm new too."

I turned my head slightly to face her. Cath – and she was new too! I could almost see a halo around her head.

"How do you know?" I asked. "I mean, about the war wound?"

"My sister told me," Cath answered. "Father Cuthbert fought in World War 1 and his leg never healed. The nuns take it in turns to dress his wound; they consider it a great privilege."

"Silence!" Sister Edward hissed and all of a sudden, I felt a fierce dig in my shoulder, causing me to stumble forwards. "This is a Holy Service! Hold your tongue, girl."

Too frightened even to turn my head to Cath, I

fixed my gaze straight ahead to the massive crucifix behind the altar, bright autumn light streaming in from the side windows onto the bare white walls. I rubbed my eyes, feeling a little strange – probably just worn out and weak from lack of sleep. No doubt I would get used to these early mornings in time.

As the service proceeded, we knelt, sat, stood and sang as one. When it was time for Communion, as I made my way up to the front of the Chapel with the rest of my row, black spots started appearing in front of my eyes and I felt fuzzy and strange.

"Are you all right?" Cath asked, her brow creasing.

"Don't know," I croaked. "I feel weird…"

"She's going!" Natalie said in a gleeful tone, as I toppled forward into the strong arms of Sister Edward.

She half-led, half-dragged me outside, my feet barely touching the ground, and sat me down on a chair with my head between my knees.

"Just a faint," she remarked. "Done this before?"

"No, never."

"You need something to eat. Wait there and I'll nip to the kitchen."

Before long I was tucking into a currant bun and slurping a cup of sweet tea with gusto, feeling like a million dollars as my grandmother would have said.

"Better?" Sister Edward asked.

I nodded.

"Fasting doesn't suit everyone," she remarked, referring to the fact that we were forbidden from eating or drinking for twelve hours before Communion. "You're lucky."

Just as I was wondering how I could be considered to be lucky to suffer from the affliction of not managing to attend a Chapel service without feeling faint, she said,

"It's harder for you, the fasting, so you've got something to offer up."

Was my face looking as blank as I felt? What did she mean?

"You can offer up your suffering to the Lord – as a penance," Sister Edward continued. "Now, I must dash back to Mass or I'll miss Communion."

"So I won't receive the Eucharist today?" I asked.

Was I to miss out on the benefits of taking Holy Communion? Was this fair, just because I was weak in body?

"You can offer that up too, the fact that you have to miss it."

I felt very pleased. This was surely going to put me in credit with the Almighty.

A little later as I queued for my breakfast in the Refectory, fellow pupils crowded round me, chattering excitedly.

"What did it feel like?"

"My sister fainted once!"

"Did you actually hit the floor?"

"Did you vomit? Did Sister Edward have to clear

it up?"

"They actually gave you a currant bun? We only have those on feast days."

I had friends, even if only for a few minutes. I was a point of interest and I fitted in – all because I had suffered. I was in credit with God too – things were definitely looking up.

"Will I always have a currant bun and tea before Chapel?" I asked the nun who was busy ladling stale cornflakes into my outstretched bowl.

She gave me an incredulous look. "We can't be busy with buns and wait on you with cups of tea every morning."

"But what if it happens again?"

"We'll see. Hopefully you won't faint again." The nun turned to the next person in the line.

"If you do faint again, you can always offer it up," Cath whispered as she made a tiny V-sign towards the unfortunate nun. I gasped at her audacity.

"Does your sister do that sort of thing?" I asked, thinking perhaps Cath had been trained to be bold at school by her sibling.

"She did," Cath replied, "until she was expelled."

The girls round me began to giggle and share their own tales of life at St Hilda's as we sat down at the tables and started munching.

Natalie entertained us with a quite frankly incredible story of how she had smuggled in her pet snake from home one term and set it loose on the Nuns' Lawn, where it promptly sank its fangs into

Reverend Mother.

Another girl recounted an astounding narrative involving running away during a school trip to hear the Bournemouth Symphony Orchestra last term; apparently, she'd only been missed once the coach was half way back to school, as the other girls had all covered for her for as long as they could, answering her name when the register had been taken. Eventually Sister Edward realised something was afoot, due no doubt to the immense amount of hysterical giggling from the girls, and the coach did a U-turn back to Bournemouth where the girl was discovered nonchalantly scoffing chips by the seafront. Now the girl was banned from any trips this term and had also received about a thousand conduct marks.

"But it was worth it," the girl explained, "because everyone knew who I was for at least a week."

"Respect!" Cath muttered under her breath. "I don't think even my sister would have thought of doing that."

I suspected the whole episode was grossly exaggerated, but it made a good story and I was enjoying the warm glow of shared discontent and insubordination. Now I knew how prisoners felt, united in their hatred of their jailors.

Maybe this would only be a brief respite from Natalie and her friends tormenting me, but I began to see a tiny glimmer of hope appearing on the horizon of misery that had been my experience since I had arrived at my new school yesterday.

Chapter 3

The first week

I felt unsettled all the first week, not quite sure what was going on. There was so much that was peculiar and even plainly bonkers, yet I was expected to assimilate it without question. For example, why did the girls talk about going to 'Mawss' instead of 'Mass'? Why was it important to say 'rum' and 'brum' instead of 'room' and 'broom'?

Why were some of the nuns called by men's names, like Sister Edward, but others had female names? And why did Reverend Mother not use her nun name, but was simply known as 'Reverend Mother', which was really a job, not a name? Why was she a 'Mother' anyway, when the other nuns were addressed as 'Sister'?

How was it possible to do a 'strip wash' every night in five minutes at our miniature pink basins, with a lukewarm flood slopping over the edges if you put so much as a flannel into the water, let alone a bar of soap? And why could we only have a bath twice a week?

Why did we have to wash our own underwear in our basins, then queue for the spin dryer, instead of chucking everything into a washing machine as our mothers did at home?

We were allowed to send larger garments to the laundry. Sadly, when the uniform shirts came back, they had been so thoroughly ironed, starched, and folded, that putting them on was a real challenge. You had to pull at the cardboard-like package with considerable force, which resulted in a shower of dried starch spraying all over the floor, then somehow soften the folds enough to bend the garment into a shape you could wear. The shirts themselves were unbelievably itchy too after the harsh treatment they'd suffered.

I sometimes felt harsh treatment of all things, whether animal, vegetable or mineral, was the order of the day at St Hilda's.

As for hair washing, I found it difficult to see why we couldn't wash our hair when it was greasy, instead of only once a week in the basins down in the Boot Room, lining up to take our turn with the communal bottle of Silvikrin.

Lessons might as well have been in a foreign language because I couldn't concentrate on a thing. Talking of foreign languages, the French teacher seemed kind, but several girls were fluent in the language already and they tended to cluster round Mam'zelle's desk, chattering away in French nineteen to the dozen, while the rest of us had to get on with dull vocabulary and ponderous grammar exercises.

Latin, I felt more confident in, until we had to

read aloud and I used a soft 'w' for the written 'v', so 'weni, widi, wici', you get the idea. This had been the way I had been taught Latin before at my previous school. To her credit, our Latin teacher struggled valiantly to explain over the guffaws of laughter that this was an equally valid way of pronunciation.

"After all," she said, "none of us know for certain exactly how the Romans spoke, it's all lost in the mists of time, so perhaps Trixie's way is the correct way?"

"Perhaps not," Natalie snorted into her text book.

I hastily resolved to change the way I read Latin texts immediately. Why make life difficult? It was bad enough already. Fitting in was important, I realised, as I turned in my seat to see Natalie almost hysterical with mirth. She was rolling her eyes and giving an impression of my pathetic attempt to read Julius Caesar's famous words to a highly diverted audience. I noticed Cath didn't join in the teasing and for that I was grateful.

We often had to sit in silence and read our library books, for example at the end of Prep, which was what our homework session was called. We were allowed to choose reading books from an approved shelf in the library, according to our year.

Cath told me there was a box of 'worthless' books we were allowed to read at weekends, but they had to be given back on Sunday evenings, whether you had finished them or not. You weren't

18

allowed to reserve your worthless book for the next weekend and would generally find it had been taken out by another girl and, despite pleading, they wouldn't let you see it. Or sometimes they would tell you the ending, 'to save you the bother of reading it'. Apparently, this had happened once too often to Cath's sister and she had punched someone on the nose when they had spoilt the ending of a 'worthless' detective novel for her, which had been another nail in the coffin on her rocky road to expulsion. Or so Cath said.

I wasn't entirely sure anymore whether to believe all the tales I had been hearing since arriving at St Hilda's; for example, Natalie's claim to be related to royalty on the wrong side of the blanket and needing to be hidden away in a convent boarding school to avoid regal embarrassment, sounded to my ears a little far-fetched and likely to have been something she'd read in one of the weekend 'worthless' books.

I was actually looking forward to next weekend in a strange sort of way so that I could sample some of these intriguing books for myself.

My worst lesson during that first week was Games. It was turning out to be a bitingly cold September and I managed to get outside without the correct kit for our first hockey lesson.

"Where are your socks?" Mrs Sidebottom the Games teacher screeched.

"My socks? I, I'm wearing socks..." I looked down

at my feet clad in my new narrow uncomfortable hockey boots, with my everyday fawn socks. Was this wrong?

"Your yellow socks," Mrs Sidebottom bawled. "Yellow socks for hockey! Take an order mark."

My eyes stung with the injustice but I said nothing. Cath gave me a lop-sided smile. The match started and I immediately managed to get struck on the head by a hockey stick.

"Foul!" Cath said. "Mrs Sidebottom! Foul! Trixie's been hit. That isn't right."

"New Bug's been injured!" Natalie crowed.

"It's only a foul if you hit someone with a stick above your shoulder," Mrs Sidebottom pronounced.

I stared round the group of girls. I was the very smallest there, in fact most of the girls towered over me. Someone lofty had managed to hit me on my head without raising their hockey stick above their shoulders, because I was so petite.

"You're unusually small," Mrs Sidebottom said, "for 12. A lot of the other girls are much better grown than you are. More mature."

One of the taller girls threw back her shoulders, displaying an impressive bosom.

"I'm 11," I said in a small voice.

"11! What are you doing in this class?" Mrs Sidebottom asked indignantly. "This is the Lower 4; it's for 12 and 13 year olds."

"And for a few 14 year olds who had to stay down a year," Natalie said spitefully.

One or two of the larger girls shuffled self-consciously to hear this circumstance mentioned.

"Must be a brain box," a voice from the back said.

"We treat everyone the same here." Mrs Sidebottom's nostrils began to flare in a spectacular fashion. "Don't think you're special just because you're a brain box and young for your class. Girls are valued for being good at sport and sewing, you know. There's more to life than books. Much more."

And with that, she blew her whistle to silence all further discussion and most of the girls pounded off down the pitch, whooping and shouting merrily.

I felt my chest tighten. Panicking, I put my head back, struggling to breath.

"You OK?" Cath asked.

"Just my asthma," I wheezed. "I get like this in the cold."

And when I was upset.

Cath looked at Mrs Sidebottom.

"Take Trixie back to school," she decided, "to Sister Edward. Then come straight back, Cath. We can't do without you in the game."

Sister Edward made me take off my bright yellow polo-neck woollen jumper so that I could breathe more easily and then put her hands round my rib cage, pressing firmly.

"In!" she commanded. "Out! Slower. You have to breathe more slowly. You're making yourself have these attacks, you know. I hear you had an asthma attack last night in your cubicle. Am I right?"

I nodded. I wanted to contradict her for saying I made myself have asthma – of course I didn't – but I couldn't manage to speak.

"You're not really ill," Sister Edward declared, standing in front of me with her arms folded. "I know what it is."

"What?" I rasped.

"You're just unhappy. You miss your parents – not really the boarding school type, are you? Try pulling yourself together."

I gulped. Yes, indeed. I needed to pull myself together pretty damn quick, otherwise I doubted whether I would be able to survive the term.

"We had a girl last year," Sister Edward continued, "and she didn't fit in – wanted to go home. We put her in The Box, because she was upsetting the other girls. She had to sleep there on her own. Now, you wouldn't like that, would you?"

I thought quickly. To me, one of the worst things about St Hilda's was that we were never, ever allowed to be on our own. I longed for the privacy and space I had always enjoyed at home.

"I, I think I would like to sleep there," I mumbled.

The Box was a tiny room above the porch in the main part of the school, just big enough for a bed, a minute wardrobe and a chair, situated not far from the library. Maybe I'd be able to stay up after official lights out if I was put in The Box? And perhaps I'd be able to sneak along to the library and borrow some books from the shelves that were out of bounds for the Lower 4s? The many benefits of not being housed right next door to Natalie in the Cubicles were worth considering too.

"What's that, Trixie? Speak up! You say you *want* to sleep there?"

I had the terrible thought then that if Sister Edward knew I wanted to sleep in The Box, she would consider I was automatically disqualified from being sent there as a punishment. Getting what you wanted was not a punishment and I suspected appropriate punishments were something the nuns thought about quite a lot. The punishment should fit the crime. And the victim.

"No, no," I wheezed. "Of course not. I meant to say, I do not, under any circumstances, want to leave the Cubicles, particularly if it means being put in a room on my own."

"And are you feeling better?"

"Yes, thank you Sister."

"Off you go then. The rest of your class will be at tea now. Hurry!"

I plodded off down the corridor and made my way to the Refectory.

When I got there, the sandwiches were all gone. I reached for a plastic tumbler of squash from the steel trolley under the watchful gaze of one of the nuns.

"Bless you, my child," she said, in a heavy Irish accent.

"I'm Trixie," I said.

"I know," she said. "And I'm Sister Anne. You're very welcome, my dear."

Cath sidled up to me and pulled a squashed jam sandwich out of her pocket.

"Managed to save one for you."

I thought I saw the ghost of a grin on Sister Anne's face as she wheeled her trolley away, limping slightly

"What's wrong with her foot?" I asked Cath.

"Nothing, as far as I know," she said. "It's just that her shoes don't fit. My sister told me Sister Anne wears the shoes girls leave behind at the end of term and they rarely fit her, so she often walks awkwardly."

There really was no end to the strangeness of this place.

A braying sound came from a group of girls nearby and I heard a few talking about 'the marks'.

"What marks are they?" I asked Cath. "I've been given a few conduct marks. Is that what they're talking about?"

"Oh no," she said. "They're mentioning the marks we've been getting in each subject. We're graded every week."

"Ah, that," I said. I vaguely remembered a few of the teachers saying I'd be getting the lowest mark possible as I hadn't handed in my work, or, in one instance, I had handed it in, but put it on the wrong shelf outside the staffroom, helpfully misdirected by Natalie and her chums.

"The marks will be up on the board in the classroom after tea," Cath said. "Oh, I hope I don't come bottom of the class. My sister came bottom once and my father cut her allowance that holiday."

We joined a stampede to the classroom as soon as we'd cleared away the cups and swept the floor free of crumbs, the corridors echoing to our shrieks and screams as we tore round the corners at breakneck speed. Where would I be placed, at the end of my first week at St Hilda's?

"You're last!" Natalie said in satisfaction as we stood in a scrum around the notice board.

"Yes, New Bug's last. Just below me," said another voice. "Makes a change not to be at the very bottom. Thank you, New Bug."

"Her name's not New Bug, it's Trixie," Cath said, "and I'm new as well."

"But you're not really new," Natalie said. "Your sister was here."

"And you're not 11," another voice said.

"Nor a midget."

"Midget! New bug! Last in the class! Midget! New bug! Last in the class!"

The chants went on until Sister Edward appeared and started bellowing.

"Girls! Stop shouting! I could hear you from the Chapel. What on earth is the matter?"

No one said anything and Sister Edward came over to look at the board.

"Not done very well in your first week, have you, Trixie?" she asked.

The rage inside me burst its dam.

"Someone has to come last," I protested. "It's like saying everyone should be above average – simply not possible. If you have a system with marks and places, someone will come last, even if their actual mark isn't that low."

"But your mark *is* low!" Sister Edward stared at me and her eyebrows bent into disapproving caterpillars. "And I don't think you'll find it very amusing when you have your mark read out in assembly on Monday morning in front of the whole school, do you?"

Chapter 4

The Box

Sister Edward was right, I didn't find it at all amusing. We assembled as usual in the Hall at the start of my second week, waiting for the Headmistress, Sister Ignatius. A few letters had been placed on the large wooden radiator cover, but not many girls seemed to have post so early in the term and there was certainly nothing for me. We had been arranged in the order of our form places, in rows forming a large horseshoe shape. When Sister Ignatius came in, silence descended, and she read out each name, mark and place is such a sour tone I thought she must have feasted on lemons for breakfast. Then unfortunately my mind went off in a flight of fancy, speculating about what the nuns did actually have for the first meal of the day, and so I totally missed the fact that I had been addressed by the Headmistress in front of the whole school.

"Trixie!" she said in acid tones. "I asked you whether you thought you had tried your best this week. Will you answer me, please? The whole school is anxious to hear your reply."

There was a collective intake of breath and many girls looked thrilled; there is genuinely nothing more exciting to the average school girl than to see someone else getting into a whole heap of trouble.

"I, I don't know whether I've tried my best," I began.

"Don't know? Do you mean you don't know what you are doing? Are you not in control of your own behaviour?" Sister Ignatius regarded me sternly, in complete disbelief. "Girls, she doesn't know whether she has tried her best. She isn't in control of herself. What do we think of this?"

I saw Sister Anne limping past the Hall through the glass door, rolling her eyes at me and I stifled a giggle before saying boldly, "Actually, I don't believe in marks and silly stuff like that. What's more, Sister Ignatius, I think you must have had a plate of lemons for breakfast to speak to me like that, I really do."

I was banished to The Box that same evening.

As I had hoped, I was pretty much left to my own devices after bedtime. Once the night nun had visited me with a strange little thick glass dish containing a wet sponge – *here my dear, make the sign of the cross with the Holy Water* – then I was free to think my own thoughts, and be my own person.

Reverend Mother had told me earlier she was contemplating ringing my parents to tell them how outrageously rude I had been in Assembly and how atrociously I had done in my academic work in my first week at St Hilda's.

Cath, however, had assured me that expulsion was unlikely to be on the cards because school numbers were low at the moment and the nuns had a business to run. I'd felt a sinking feeling to hear this, realising I would not be escaping back to my parents anytime soon, more's the pity.

To cheer myself up, I decided to risk a trip to the library after lights out, not something I would ever have contemplated from the Cubicles. Opening my door carefully, I saw the corridor duty nun snoozing gently in her chair, her prayer book tilted sideways; creeping along, I tried to judge as best I could which creaking floorboards to avoid, feeling my way along the dim passageway to the library. The door knob was stiff but I managed to turn it without a sound and sneak inside. I had a tiny torch which I had brought from home and kept hidden in my toiletry bag, and I used it to scan the shelves. Totally ignoring the Lower 4 shelf, I soon found something much more interesting – *War and Peace* – tucking it under my arm before retreating back to The Box. So far, so good. I managed to read three chapters before weariness overcame me and I fell asleep, untroubled by thoughts of my poor behaviour, my parents or home, so caught up in Tolstoy's world had I become.

I woke very early the next morning when I heard a car coming up the drive. Peering out of the tiny metal framed window with diamond panes next to my bed, I could see a taxi. Who on earth could it be at this hour? I released the catch and stuck my head out. A tall figure in jeans and a leather jacket climbed out of the car. I sneaked out of my room in my nightie and looked over the wide staircase, trying to find out what was going on.

"On time, good." Sister Ignatius' voice floated up the stairs to me. "Hope he remembers not to ring the bell."

The sharp squeal of a bolt being pulled open echoed up the stairs, followed by the creaking protest of the front door hinges.

"Welcome!" I heard Sister Ignatius' voice again, this time with a strangely friendly tone, almost as if she was greeting a family member, not a mysterious stranger arriving at an unusually early hour.

I withdrew to my room, anxious not to be discovered, tingling with questions. Why would someone arrive so early? What business would a young man have in a convent? Why wouldn't Sister Ignatius have wanted him to ring the bell? Who was he, anyway?

I was too curious to attempt to sleep again, so sat up with my book until the sixth former on duty flung the door open.

"Morning! Time to get up! Benedicamus Domine!"

Her eyes nearly popped out of her head to see me reading. "Crikey! What's that?"

"*War and Peace*."

"Rather you than me – brain box!" she said as she clattered off on her way.

A minute later she appeared again at the door.

"You do know you're supposed to answer 'Deo Gracias' when I say 'Benedicamus Domine', don't you?"

"Is it compulsory?" I attempted a half-smile.

The sixth former sniggered. "I'd say advisable rather than compulsory."

"Any more words of wisdom?"

"Don't let the nuns find you reading! I say, Trixie, we all thought you were awfully brave to say what you did yesterday, to Sister Ignatius."

"Really? Didn't you think I was an idiot?"

"Well, maybe that as well. But mostly brave. Chop, chop now – don't be late for Chapel."

Chapel! I pulled on my clothes after a desultory attempt at washing and said a quick prayer begging that I might not faint again this morning.

Sadly, my petition went unanswered and I was carted out of the service yet again by Sister Edward and left on a chair with my head down, a cup of sweet tea by my side.

No currant bun this morning. I expect they didn't want to encourage me.

This was how I happened to be in the corridor when the mysterious stranger I had seen that morning appeared again. He was now clad in black and would have been considered handsome but for the ferocious scowl fixed on his face, which quite spoilt his features.

"Who are you?" he demanded. "I was told it was safe to have a look around as there wouldn't be anyone about."

"I'm no one. A New Bug. I'm a fainter too, so I've been let off the rest of the service."

His face softened and he attempted a grin.

"I'm Father Tom," he said, holding out his hand.

"How do you do?" I answered.

"Hey, better put your head down again," he cautioned. "Beginning to look a bit green around the gills."

"Why are you here?" I said from under the chair.

"I'm the new chaplain," he said.

I thought this couldn't possibly be true, as if he was, he would have attended the service along with the rest of the school, but I decided it would be rude to challenge him.

"Is Father Cuthbert leaving?" I asked.

"Not exactly. He's just going to take things a bit more easily, sort of semi-retirement – I'll be here to help out."

Sounded reasonable, but something didn't quite stack up.

"I saw you arrive," I said. "Early this morning. My room is directly over the front door."

"You did?" He twisted his hands together. "Perhaps you shouldn't say anything about that. And also, if you can, please don't mention to your friends that you've seen me here in the corridor. They'll be told about my arrival in the fullness of time."

"I haven't exactly got a lot of friends to tell, apart from Cath." I was sitting up again by now, sipping my tea. "Comes from being the New Bug."

"You'll settle in; always take a bit of time."

"And I was very badly behaved in assembly yesterday..." I started before he interrupted me with,

"Good God! You're the one – I've heard all about you from Sister Ignatius."

I tried to look ashamed but failed miserably.

"You've a damn cheek!" he said.

Did I detect a touch of admiration in his tone?

"You were pretty rude to Sister Ignatius," he said. "She's my aunt, by the way. Bet you didn't know that."

He may have been Sister Ignatius' nephew – there was no reason for him to lie about that – but I still wasn't sure he was a priest because I didn't think a man of God would use the language he was using. I looked at his feet. Shoes were always a dead giveaway. People don't always realise it, but your shoes often say a great deal about who you really are.

I stared. He was wearing boots, and not just any boots, but really quite fashionable ankle boots with a zip up the side, and they were brown, which didn't match his priestly outfit of black. And when he had arrived earlier, he had been wearing jeans and a leather jacket, so he must have changed his clothes since then, but not his boots, which didn't seem to add up. All in all, I decided that no way was he a priest. And I bet he wasn't here just to help Father Cuthbert either, even though Father Cuthbert had a war wound and was finding his job a bit tough. That must be some sort of excuse.

"Does Reverend Mother know?" I asked. "I presume Sister Ignatius knows, if she's your aunt."

"Know what?"

"That you're not a priest."

Father Tom let out a long slow whistle. "Sharp, aren't you?" His mouth curved into a smile.

I looked up to his eyes because they say if the smile doesn't reach the eyes, you're in trouble, but at that very moment the Chapel doors were flung open and hordes of girls eager for their breakfast flooded out. Father Tom, or whoever he was, simply disappeared and I was left not knowing whether that smile was genuine or not. Or whether I'd spoken out of turn enough to get me into severe trouble. Again.

A shiver ran down my back. This was so exciting! We had an intruder in our midst masquerading as a priest, and he was Sister Ignatius' nephew. Did the other nuns know? I presumed he would be introduced to the school at some point as the new chaplain, but for some reason, not quite yet. Maybe he had a few tasks to do first? Like getting some more suitable footwear?

My heart raced as I considered all the possibilities. Perhaps he was in hiding, a witness to a crime? Or maybe he was an undercover policeman disguised as a priest, although that wouldn't explain him being Sister Ignatius' nephew, because she'd have had to know...oh dear, this was getting very muddled.

He could be investigating the other nuns for something or other. Maybe fraud? Unlikely. Receiving stolen property? There did seem to be quite a lot of gold and silver items on the altar.

I had heard there were some girls at the school from very wealthy families; could it be possible that he was here to guard them? A threat could have been made to their lives; they could have a vast sum on their heads and be in danger of kidnap...

"Trixie!" It was Cath. "Come on, slow coach! It's breakfast. I've saved you some fried bread. Follow me."

I trotted after my new best friend, feeling for the first time since my arrival that I was going to find plenty to do at this strange place that was to be my home for the next six years.

Chapter 5

Father Tom and Sister Anne

A couple of days later, on a particularly fine September morning, Reverend Mother had a special announcement to make in Assembly. She clapped her hands and beamed.

"Allow me to introduce Father Tom, our new chaplain, an assistant to Father Cuthbert."

"Aren't we blessed, girls," Sister Ignatius had added to Reverend Mother's statement, "blessed in the extreme to have been granted TWO chaplains?"

A murmur of assent ran round the Hall and everyone looked thrilled to have a new face to look at, particularly a young male face.

"Look! One of his buttons is loose."

"He's tall, isn't he?"

"Not as tall as my father..."

"Do you think black suits him?"

I felt sorry for Father Tom then. He flushed beetroot red and started swinging his arms back and forth, rather like a gorilla. Further evidence, in my book, that he wasn't really a chaplain, because he seemed unused to the forensic level of scrutiny shown in every detail of his appearance.

I was interested to notice he'd abandoned his brown boots and was sporting a pair of battered black lace-ups that looked too big for him, possibly belonging originally to Father Cuthbert, who had large feet, at least a size 12.

Meanwhile the comments continued unabated.

"He looks about forty-four."

"Ancient!"

"No, he's much younger – maybe thirty?"

"Twenty? Same age as that pop star..."

"Silence!" Sister Edward roared. "Silence! Young ladies do not make this much noise. Do they?"

No one dared to answer this menacing question and Sister Edward's hooded eyes smouldered, fixing on the characters she thought had been most at fault. Her gaze lingered on me for ages, which I thought unfair.

"Would you like to address the girls, Father?" Reverend Mother asked. "Say a prayer?"

Father Tom took a step back, looking petrified and as if he would rather be anywhere than in St Hilda's Hall being stared at by hordes of adolescent girls. He gulped noisily, causing a ripple of instantly suppressed laughter from some of the bolder creatures in the sixth form.

"Y, yes..." he stammered. "Let us pray."

"Bow your heads, girls," Sister Ignatius snapped.

"Yes, and that means you too, Trixie," Sister Edward added.

We all inspected the highly polished floor. I

could see a tiny earwig creeping into a crack in the wide honey-coloured boards, obviously as desperate to melt away as Father Tom was.

"Let us pray a special prayer," Father Tom started, "a special new prayer, one that I have composed just for today, right now in fact, for this remarkable occasion. Lord, help us all to seek the truth, to ask and find answers, to investigate and to lay bare what should be known."

Cath was standing next to me and she started to tremble violently, as did a few other girls. Using the word 'bare' was bound to provoke merriment at St Hilda's.

Father Tom finished hastily with the sign of the cross and mercifully it was time for us to be released for lessons.

As we pounded the corridors, Sister Edward shrieked, "Girls! Remember how to behave!"

I wondered if I should tell Cath of my suspicions about Father Tom not being quite who he said he was. She'd become a good friend in a remarkably short time, but I was wary of putting my trust in her until I knew her better. No, I'd keep my own counsel for now. But I would also keep my wits about me and see if I could find out what was really going on.

Sister Anne was waiting for me in The Box when I finally made my way up to my room at the end of a long and weary day. When I say waiting for me, that doesn't give the whole picture. She was actually hiding behind the door, and it was all I could do not to scream out in startled terror when I noticed her.

"Hush my child!" she said. "Don't be alarmed."

"Sister Anne," I squeaked. "You scared me half to death."

She smiled and I realised she was far younger than I'd previously thought. The nuns all tended to look pretty much the same to us, hidden away in their long old-fashioned habits with little capes disguising their figures and full veils and wimples concealing every scrap of hair. The way we talked about them, you could be forgiven for thinking that they were all in their nineties, although I'm pretty sure quite a few of them were. But here was Sister Anne, fresh-faced and enthusiastic, looking for all the world as if she were barely out of her teens.

"You, you seem different," I stammered. "And you sound English. What's happened to your Irish accent?"

She took a step towards me. "Hush. Someone's coming!"

Quick as a flash she flung herself under my narrow bed in the nick of time, just before a nun creaked into the room holding the holy water dish.

"Is it that time already?" I asked. "I must get ready for bed."

"Sleep well, my child," the ancient nun said. "I must away to the dormitories now; I can hear the girls cavorting and having fun. So sorry you have to be here alone. I hope you're not too lonely?"

"Not at all," I assured her.

As soon as she'd gone, Sister Anne leapt out from under the bed.

"Your leg!" I cried. "You're not limping any more. Have you been given some new shoes?"

"Have I *what*?"

"We all know you're so unworldly that you only wear the shoes girls leave behind at the end of term and they don't fit you, so you limp."

When Sister Anne had finished wiping tears of hilarity from her eyes, she sat down on the bed.

"Listen," she said, "I can't begin to imagine who told you that complete pack of lies. Truth is, sometimes it suits me to limp. Just as it occasionally suits me to put on an Irish accent. And other accents too...I do a wonderful Italian. If I hadn't wanted to become a nun, I would have been an actress."

"An actress! Wow!"

I was impressed.

"Yes! And I would have changed my name to something much more glamorous than Anne, I can tell you. Sophia, or Esmerelda, maybe Petunia...?"

"Is Anne your real name then? I thought when you became a nun, you took a saint's name."

"Yes, but Anne is a saint's name already, so I thought I would keep it as a nun; I thought it was suitable, being plain. I certainly didn't want to change my name to a man's name, like Sister Edward and Sister Ignatius." Sister Anne fiddled with the edge of her cape. "Have you met Sister Phoebe yet?"

"Not exactly met, but I know who she is," I replied. "I've seen her in Chapel. She's the tiny one who does the laundry, isn't she?"

"That's it! She chose the name Phoebe when she took the veil; her parents called her Gertrude and she often says she hated that name so much that she decided as a small child she'd become a nun so that she could change it."

"She sounds quite a character," I said. "I look forward to meeting her properly."

"Yes, indeed. She's super, and moreover, you can trust her. Now, you need to get ready for bed, in case anyone else comes to check on you, then I want you to meet us outside, near the huts at the back of the Hall. Don't forget to leave a pile of clothes heaped up in your bed to look as if you're fast asleep."

I rubbed my eyes. Any minute now, I'd have to pinch myself too, because surely to goodness I must be dreaming. Wait, what was it she had said?

"Us?" I asked. "Who do you mean by 'us'?"

"Why, Father Tom and me. There's so much you don't know yet. All will be revealed. See you in about half an hour?"

With that, she flew out of the room, slamming the door behind her, then had to return to release her veil from where it had become trapped in the door.

"Pesky thing," she remarked. "Still getting used to wearing all this clobber."

Curiouser and curiouser. I undressed in a hurry and completed my strip wash and teeth cleaning in a flash. Lying on the bed, I pondered yet again how very lucky I was to have a room to myself. This sort of adventure would be much more difficult if I was still in the Cubicles, with Natalie and the others all too well aware of my every movement. You couldn't even turn the pages of a book there without everyone else hearing and thinking you were a weird brain box. I sighed as I thought of my reading. *War and Peace* was getting to a very exciting part and it would be a shame to miss out, but on the other hand, it sounded as if I was going to have a big adventure of my own tonight, meeting up with Sister Anne and Father Tom.

Hearing a sound, I peered out of the window and saw the nuns' Mini racing up the drive, its headlights illuminating the stone walls. It screeched to a halt and Sister Phoebe crept out, the most diminutive nun in the convent. They said when she drove, she could scarcely see out of the windscreen; apparently, she'd been stopped for speeding quite a few times but the police always let her off when she offered to say the rosary for their sins. Everyone likes the thought of being in credit with the Almighty; I suppose it was a bit like the Medieval Church, when the Pope sold indulgences to the faithful.

Sister Phoebe scuttled to the front door, and

then I could see her no more, although I could definitely hear someone on the stairs so I lay down and pulled the covers over me.

At last, all was quiet; I arranged my games kit into a Trixie-sized lump and pulled the bed covers over it, then made my way along the corridor. I didn't want to risk using the main staircase – there was literally nowhere to hide – so I melted along the corridor, past the library, to where the old Victorian House joined with a more modern extension, and inched down the lino-covered staircase to the ground floor. It was easy then to make my way outside and run past the Refectory, through the paved section and out onto the field, crossing the drive and leaping through a wooded area until I reached the huts at the back of the Hall. I did hope my slippers weren't getting too muddy.

"We thought you'd never get here," Sister Anne said.

"I had to wait until it was all quiet, then I went the long way round to avoid being seen."

Father Tom grinned at me. "At your service Trixie," he said with a flourish, as he pretended to doff his non-existent cap.

"Come on," Sister Anne said. "Stop messing around! Explain what it is we want Trixie to do, then she can get back to bed."

"We want you to help," Father Tom said. "Is that all right? You've obviously guessed that I'm not quite who I say I am."

"So, are you an undercover cop?" I asked eagerly.

Sister Anne frowned. "Do you watch a lot of television?"

"Undercover policeman?" I corrected myself.

"Guilty as charged," Father Tom said. "Sister Ignatius really is my aunt, but so far she is the only nun who knows that I'm also a policeman."

"But Sister Anne knows," I said. "And she's a nun."

"I'm a novice, not a full nun yet," Sister Anne said. "I'm still in training; there are years to go before I take my final vows."

"Oh, don't take them," I begged. "You'll have a better life if you leave the convent. Are you sure you want to give up on love and marriage, and stuff like babies, when you're so young?"

"Trixie!" Sister Anne pulled her collar straight and lifted her chin. "I think that's my decision, don't you?"

Father Tom began to laugh.

"See!" I said. "He agrees with me."

"I'm not saying whether I agree or disagree. It'd be more than my life's worth. Anyway, Trixie, the thing is, Sister Anne and I have a sort of bond between us."

I looked up eagerly. "You mean you like each other?"

"Not exactly," he said. "Oh, well, of course we like each other, but that's..."

"Irrelevant?" Sister Anne suggested.

"Yes, irrelevant."

She was finishing his sentences. That meant

they were in tune with each other. Could they be in love? I let this idea roll around my mind for a little while as I bit my lip. All the books I had read, even the classics, especially the classics, had love at the centre and maybe real life would be no different...

"Trixie!" Sister Anne was frowning now.

"The bond between us is professional," Father Tom said. "Sister Anne is helping me investigate a mystery. In fact, it was she who first flagged up the suspicion that something was wrong at St Hilda's."

"Yes indeed," she burst in. "I became convinced that there were strangers lurking in the bushes and trees on the drive. I've got very good eyesight, unlike many of the older nuns – once I distinctly saw a male figure running over the Nuns' Lawn, but when I mentioned it to Sister Edward, who was with me at the time, she said my mind might have been playing tricks. I told Sister Ignatius and she seemed slightly more concerned – perhaps she was worried about security? That's when she called Tom, who as you know is her nephew, and he offered to come to the convent and see what he could discover. Sister Ignatius asked me to liaise with Tom and the two of us have her permission to carry out an investigation into whatever is, or is not, going on."

"Have there been any other sightings, or un-usual occurrences?" I asked.

I had read a lot of Agatha Christie.

"There was the digging," Father Tom said. "Don't forget the shadowy figure you saw with a spade one night at the end of the summer, under the Witch's Finger."

"That was highly suspicious," Sister Anne said. "I told Sister Ignatius about that too, but she said it was probably nothing, in fact she was adamant that I must have been mistaken."

Father Tom, or Policeman Tom, frowned to hear this. Interesting.

"The Witch's Finger!" I said. "Cath showed me that tree only yesterday."

"Thing is, Trixie," Father Tom continued, "we want you to be our eyes and ears. Will you help us?"

"Yes," Sister Anne said. "Now you have been banished to sleep in The Box, you have the ideal vantage point to spy on the drive."

"It's a deal!" I said.

This was more like it – something to get my teeth into and relieve the tedium of daily life at St Hilda's.

"Could you make notes?" Father Tom asked. "Jot down what you see? Any intruders or visitors, that sort of thing."

"But don't put yourself in any danger," Sister Anne warned. "Just observe and keep a record."

"How do I report back?" I asked.

"I'm coming to that," Father Tom said. "But first, promise me you're OK with this. Are you in?"

"I'm in!" I whispered.

This was totally thrilling!

"And listen carefully to what's going on, too,"

Sister Anne said. "Maybe some of the other girls might see something or someone unusual."

"But don't let them know it's of any significance," Tom said. "Just write it down and then..."

"Leave it up there." Sister Anne pointed to the gothic turret at the side of St Hilda's. "You can get into the Tower from the main part of the Hall, through the side door, also from the huts, through the Boot Room and the Undercroft. There's a small loose stone at the top of the stairs, about the height of your shoulder. Pull it out and there's a recess where you can hide your notes."

"Thank you," I murmured.

"You don't have to thank us," Father Tom said. "We should be thanking you."

"Oh, but I do, have to thank you, I mean," I replied. "I've got something important to occupy me at last. It's going to be so much fun – can't wait!"

"Scamper back to bed then," Sister Anne said. "Hope you sleep well."

As I ran off, retracing my steps, I glanced back and saw the two of them standing very close to each other; Father Tom had his arm on Sister Anne's sleeve and seemed to be asking her something.

I felt annoyed I didn't possess supersonic hearing but didn't allow it to spoil my happiness at my new mission in life. I had a purpose! I was part of a team and I was jolly well going to be the best detective it was possible to be.   ·

Chapter 6

Looking for clues

As soon as I got back to The Box that evening, I dug out a tiny notebook I had brought from home, and wrote my name in it, and 'Top Secret!' on the front.

I settled down in bed, but sleep eluded me. Looking out of the window, I saw two mysterious figures moving across the drive, keeping well within the shadows of the trees. I reached for my notebook. Ah. It was only Father Tom and Sister Anne. I could recognise them now they'd got a bit closer. They seemed to be talking to each other, then Father Tom melted away, no doubt on his way to Father Cuthbert's quarters in the Clock Tower where he was lodging. Sister Anne stood quite still and seemed to be looking up at my window. I raised my hand tentatively, but she didn't respond, or not as far as I could see. I rubbed my eyes; must be tired.

Then Anne made her way back across the top of the drive and round behind the Hall. I wondered if she might be going to climb the Tower, but before I could wonder why, I started drifting into a deep sleep.

The next day I was keen to look for clues and mysterious strangers, but frustratingly there was nothing to report and my notebook remained blank. Just as well, because it slipped out of my pocket in a science lesson and was immediately pounced on by Natalie.

"Look!" she crowed. "Trixie's got a secret notebook. Let's have a look – what's she written about us?"

She flicked through the pages, then lost interest when she found nothing there and discarded the notebook under her bench. I managed to retrieve it at the end of the lesson and stuff it back in my pocket.

I thought she'd forgotten all about it, but found on the way into Chapel the next morning a hot whisper behind me said, "Trixie's a spy!" I knew it was Natalie, although when I turned round, she had assumed a 'butter wouldn't melt' sort of expression. Her speciality.

On Sunday, as it was a very wet autumn afternoon, we were all rounded up in the Hall.

"Anyone want to play jacks?" Natalie asked.

Jacks were a craze at the time. Lots of girls owned a set of the little metal shapes and a small red rubber ball, and used to while away the hours challenging each other to games, which turned into massive tournaments if the rain kept up for long enough.

"I'll play!" Cath said. She skidded across the highly polished floor and landed on her knees next to Natalie who was busy spilling jacks out of a tiny cloth bag. We all gathered round eagerly.

"Cath! I know you'll win."

"Natalie! Natalie! Come ON!"

"I'll play the winner!"

"Me next!"

Cath looked as if she was going to make it to the next round, so skilful was she at swiping the jacks up while the ball bounced, but Natalie managed to put her off her stride by pointing out that her hair had split ends and her nose was too large for her face, which the rest of us thought was unfair, even if it was true.

"You next, Trixie," Natalie said. "I'm going to murder you."

I shuffled forward and started to play but it wasn't really my thing. I couldn't co-ordinate the throwing of the jacks, and the bouncing and catching of the ball properly, and when I swiped my hand across the floor to pick up the jacks, I felt a stabbing pain.

"Oh no!" Cath said. "That's a nasty splinter – you have to make sure you move in the direction of the grain of the wood because this floor can be lethal."

"What's going on?" Sister Edward said. "Who's making a fuss?"

"Trixie is!" Natalie squealed.

"She's got a really massive splinter," Cath explained.

"Mm." Sister Edward inspected my throbbing finger. "That is most impressive. I happen to have a pin here in my pocket."

"Pin! Pin! Pin!" The excited shouts echoed round the Hall.

Sister Edward grabbed my finger and was just about to use the rusty pin to dig the piece of wood out when Sister Anne appeared.

"Here, let me help you, Sister," she said. "I'll take Trixie over to the window. The light's better there. Oh, it's no trouble. I'll have that out in no time."

My heart restored its normal rhythm and I found myself alone with Sister Anne in the large bay window, the others having lost interest and started the next game of jacks.

"Have you found out anything?" Sister Anne said as she very gently worked the splinter loose. "I did take a look in the Tower to see if you had left us a note, but there was nothing there."

"I haven't seen a thing," I confessed.

"Here! That wasn't so bad, was it?" Sister Anne showed me the tiny jagged piece of wood that had caused all the trouble, now lying flat on the tip of her finger. "Time these floorboards were sanded down."

"All done?" Sister Edward barked.

"Yes, thank you Sister," I said.

"Back to the game of jacks then," she commanded.

"Might I have permission to read?" I asked.

"It's not reading time. It's socialising time. You

make friends for life here, never forget that. The girls at St Hilda's will always be your best friends, wherever you go."

I looked at the group of girls competing fiercely over a few scraps of metal and a red ball and sighed – then had a brainwave.

"Sister Edward! I don't know if you know this, but I learn the piano – would it be possible for me to go and practise?"

I knew that almost the only way to be by yourself at this strange school was if you were either banished to The Box, or learnt an instrument. Most of the girls hated practising and did all they could to get out of their sessions, but I could already see that I was going to become very fond of music; it would enable me to have peace and quiet away from the incessant high spirits and general boisterous shrieking that seemed a characteristic of life at St Hilda's.

"Of course you may go and practise, my dear," Sister Edward said. "Make sure you spend sufficient time on your scales; they are hard work but you won't regret it."

"Thank you," I said and glanced at Sister Anne who was smiling broadly.

"And Trixie," Sister Edward called after me.

"Yes, Sister Edward?"

"You are really turning a corner. Your handwriting practice was almost creditable this week and I noticed you managed not to faint this morning in Chapel. Well done! Keep this up and you'll soon be back in the Cubicles. You've been punished long enough in The Box."

I dragged my feet as I left the Hall, realising what this would mean. No longer would I be able to sit up reading till all hours, or spy on the front door and drive. Also, it had to be said, the only reason I hadn't fainted this morning in Chapel was because I'd had something to eat before the service; I'd managed to pinch a piece of bread on the way out of the Refectory last night by shoving it up my sleeve when the nuns weren't looking. When I say bread, I'm referring to the white pappy stuff we all called 'Mother's Shame' instead of 'Mother's Pride'. It had tasted a bit odd and stale this morning, but anything was better than fainting.

As I made my way along the empty corridors, lit by wholly inadequate single light bulbs, the gloomy feel of autumn permeated into my very bones. What there was to look forward to?

Christmas, a small voice said inside me. You can look forward to Christmas, because that's the next time you'll see your parents.

I was due to spend half term in Devon, because it was just too far to travel to Italy to join my parents merely for one week. I was sure my time in the South West with my aunt and uncle would be lovely but it wouldn't the same as being at home with Mum and Dad. I pushed my shoulders back, determined not to feel sorry for myself. Why, I would have a great time, and this afternoon I had managed to escape from the Hall and the mind-numbing games of jacks. Even Christmas wasn't so far away...

I spent a happy half hour after that in the company of Bach and Mozart, then packed up my music books and returned to the Hall, where Sister Edward had everyone standing in two parallel lines.

"Scottish dancing," she announced. "We're all going to dance some reels. I'll just start the music..."

As Sister Edward bent over a cherry-red box record player and the needle made that irritating hissing and crackling before the jaunty music started, Sister Anne caught my eye and beckoned me over to the other side of the Hall. No one had even noticed I'd returned, so I sidled over and followed her out of the far door to the winding stone staircase and down to the Boot Room where Father Tom was waiting for us.

Chapter 7

Midnight swim

"I haven't found out anything," I apologised. "I'm a useless spy. You'd be better off without me."

"Not at all," Father Tom said. "Even the fact that you haven't seen anything tells its own story."

He was generous to say this. Surely it would have been better if I'd seen all sorts of shenanigans and had a full dossier to put in the special hiding place in the Tower?

"Really," he insisted.

"You're doing great," Sister Anne said. "You're in place for when we need you."

"Just one problem, though..." I began.

"I know!" she cut in. "You're probably going to be moved back to the Cubicles very soon from The Box. I heard what Sister Edward said earlier. Don't look so sad, Trixie. I'll help you move your stuff back to the Cubicles."

"But in fact, that's going to be perfect," Father Tom said, "because Sister Anne noticed something up at the Laundry yesterday."

"Yes, it was very weird," Sister Anne said. "I thought I saw someone creeping about behind the building when I went for my evening stroll; I was in the field nearby and admittedly I couldn't get a very clear view, but it looked like quite a thick-set, squat figure..."

Goodness! This could change the course of our investigation – although, to be fair, thick-set and squat described several of the nuns quite well.

"So, what do you want me to do?" I asked.

"Well, some of the girls in your class are planning a midnight swim tonight," Sister Anne said, leaning forward. "I heard them talking about it during one of those endless games of jacks this afternoon – we want you to go along too."

"Yes," Father Tom said. "It's the perfect cover. You can snoop around the Laundry on the way up to the pool. There'll be safety in numbers. Just look out for clues near the building, maybe a cigarette butt, footprints, something like that."

"I haven't got a costume," I said, ever practical. "The uniform list didn't mention a swimming costume for the autumn term."

"Yes, that's correct," Sister Anne said. "There's isn't any official swimming this term as the pool is open air and completely freezing – sorry about that. But the other girls in your class will have brought their cossies as midnight swimming is all the rage."

I wrinkled my nose. "Isn't it forbidden?"

"No," she said. "The other nuns don't know it goes on, so they can't forbid it; that means that technically, it's not against the rules. And you'll be pleased to know I've taken a swimming costume out of lost property for you; here we are – looks about your size."

Sister Anne produced a bright green nylon garment from a deep pocket of her habit. "See? It's from Poyntz House – you're in that house, aren't you? Not that it probably matters if you wear the colour from another house, but I like to get things right, and besides, I think the green will suit you."

"Are you sure you're entirely suited to being a nun," I joked, "what with eavesdropping, encouraging girls to go for midnight swims, taking things from lost property without permission, worrying about the colours of swimsuits and so on..."

My voice trailed off and I looked at the couple in front of me, who were gazing at each other in a very soppy fashion. Maybe there were other reasons why Sister Anne wasn't suited to convent life and wouldn't be taking her final vows, and of course Father Tom wasn't exactly a real priest. My over-active imagination bounded ahead as usual and very soon I was walking up an aisle in a country church dressed in a spriggy bridesmaid's dress behind Sister Anne, while Father Tom, or just plain Tom, was waiting for his beloved at the altar...

Father Tom cleared his throat. "Ahem! To the point. Would you mind not bothering with taking notes on this occasion, Trixie?"

"Sure," I said. "But I don't want to forget anything."

"We know Natalie found your notebook in the

science lesson," Sister Anne said, "and we can't risk anything being found."

"How did you know about that?" I asked.

"I was in the prep room helping to mix chemicals when you were having your science lesson," Sister Anne said, "and I saw what went on."

"It's hard to keep a secret in this place," Father Tom said. "The walls seem to have ears."

I looked at him, standing in front of me, his fingertips lightly brushing Sister Anne's and a fit of giggles threatened to overwhelm me as I thought how much I agreed with him. It was indeed very hard to keep a secret at St Hilda's. I could only hope no one else had noticed their growing closeness. A thought struck me then that perhaps the two of them hadn't quite twigged how fond they obviously were of each other. Yet! Only a matter of time in my opinion – although it would be true to say that everything I knew about romance had come from between the covers of a book, so it was quite possible I had the wrong idea about one or two things.

"Now," Sister Anne said, "if you think you can manage it without getting too tired, meet us by the Witch's Finger after swimming this evening and report anything you've seen."

"Yes – does that sound OK?" Father Tom said. "And maybe don't mention this to your friend Cath yet."

"Sure." Hopefully it wouldn't be too long before I could confide in Cath.

"Better get back," Sister Anne said. "You'll be just in time for the next reel – I can hear the introduction being played."

I scampered up the steps and crept into the Hall again, melting into a line of over-excited dancers as a Scottish reel blared out from the record player.

"Beautiful, girls!" Sister Edward yelled. "Keep those lines straight. That's it!"

"Where have you been?" Cath quizzed me.

"Piano practice," I said.

"But you came in from the door at the back and you were gone for such a long time."

"Went the long way round," I said, which was sort of true. Then I added, "I love playing Bach on the piano and being by myself for a while, like I used to at home," which was definitely true.

As Sister Anne had predicted, I was told to move back to the Cubicles very soon, in fact that very evening. Sister Anne was as good as her word and helped me to move my belongings. She even made my bed for me.

After lights out, a group of us sneaked out of the Cubicles wearing swimming costumes under our nighties. We'd decided to wear outdoor shoes, not our slippers, as muddy slippers could have led to unwelcome questions in the morning if the nuns had seen them, whereas muddy shoes would merely lead to the usual request to, "Go to the Boot Room and get those shoes really clean. Remember you are a young lady and people judge you by your shoes. What would someone think if the first time they met you, you had dirty shoes? What sort of impression would that make?" and so on, ad infinitum.

We made our way across the courtyard and round the back of the Science Block, trying hard not to crunch on the gravel. Cath gave a little scream at one point and thought she had seen 'something weird and nasty' fly past, but I explained it was probably only a bat. She didn't seem reassured, but instead clung to my arm so fiercely I began to think her fingers would leave bruises.

Natalie led the way. As we marched past the Laundry on our right, she turned to face her followers.

"I say! Wouldn't it be the most tremendous fun if we broke into the Laundry and threw some detergent powder onto the floor or jumped on some freshly washed clothes?"

Even for Natalie, this was mean. Sister Phoebe, the laundry nun, was held in very high esteem by the majority of pupils; she seemed to do most of the washing and ironing of uniforms for the whole school, no small feat with over two hundred girls.

Natalie peered through the window, as if trying to assess whether she could be bothered to go in, then leapt in alarm.

"Run," she shrieked. "Run! Meet you all by the big oak over there."

We raced after her, breathless and confused. Once we were safely hiding behind the tree, she said, "There was someone in there! Must have been Sister Phoebe. Hope she doesn't report us."

We bowed our heads and felt even more sorry for Sister Phoebe. Ten o'clock at night was very late to be still doing manual labour, even for a nun, although it must take a lot of time to wash, starch and iron the shirts in her special way and fold them into cardboard shapes.

"I'm going to try and keep my clothes as clean as I can," Cath said, "so that Sister Phoebe has less work to do."

"Me too!" said another voice, and in no time at all, most of us had pledged to be more careful with ink and food, the two substances we managed to mess up our uniforms with most days, so that poor Sister Phoebe could have less of a burden.

But then I had a different thought. It was more logical to think that Sister Phoebe was safely tucked up in her bed in the Nuns' Quarters by now, or at least maybe sipping some cocoa and reading a book about the Lives of the Saints in the Nun's Common Room. Could the figure hiding in the Laundry be one of the mysterious strangers Sister Anne thought she'd seen? Maybe the person she'd spied digging near the Witch's Finger last summer?

I felt a thrill shoot through me, then we all ran after Natalie, continuing on and on, way up to the end of the field, past the hockey pitch and beyond. The swimming pool was about as far away from the main school as you could get. We would be able to laugh and swim and play around without fear of being detected. It never once crossed our minds that if we got into any sort of trouble in the water, getting cramp or some other difficulty, we would not be able to be rescued.

We were soon having fun in the pool, bobbing about holding polystyrene floats; Natalie kept trying to hold my head under the water 'for a lark', but I managed to get away by swimming off to the deep end.

"Eek! It's cold," Cath screamed as she lay on her back.

"Keep moving," I urged.

"Yes," another girl said. "Keep waggling your legs and you won't get frostbite."

"Get out of the pool right now, unless you want to get hurt," a low voice said.

"That's not Father Cuthbert," Cath said.

"No, nor Father Tom," Natalie added.

The accent was Australian, and the tone rough; it was a voice none of us had ever heard before, and, judging from the terrified splashing and screeching echoing round the pool, a voice none of us ever wanted to hear again.

"Is that you messing about, Natalie?" Cath asked.

"No!" she squeaked.

"It's physically impossible for any one of us to have a bass voice," I said.

The screaming rose in intensity; we were terrified.

"There's no one to hear you," the menacing voice boomed and a shadowy male figure appeared next to the pool edge. "Far too isolated up here. Don't you dare tell a living soul about seeing me up here tonight, or you'll regret it and that's a promise. Now, clear off back to bed, the lot of you, before I lose my temper and do something horrible. And keep quiet, will you – that screaming's doing my head in."

The man had already lost his temper, but instead of pointing this out to him, we took his advice and scarpered back to the Cubicles as quickly as possible. No one made any attempt to look in at the Laundry on the way back, or to try to avoid crunching on the gravel. We pushed and stumbled our way to the safety of our beds, some still barefoot and many without their belongings. There would have to be a retrieval operation in the morning before daybreak, or awkward questions would be asked.

It did not occur to any of us to alert the nuns that there was an intruder on the premises; most of the girls were too scared by what the man had said and also too worried about being ticked off for midnight swimming, although I had pointed out a few times it was still only about eleven o'clock, nowhere near midnight.

I lay motionless on my bed, waiting for the others to fall asleep, anxious to set off for my assignation with Tom and Anne by the Witch's Finger. I had already decided in my mind that the next time

I saw them I would call them Tom and Anne, not Father Tom and Sister Anne – it seemed crazy to go on calling them by names that didn't truly describe who they were, for Tom wasn't a priest and Anne wasn't yet a full nun. And she probably never would be, the way things were going.

Ten minutes later I put my school coat on; it was a very itchy Harris Tweed sack, but I thought I would be glad of the warmth as I had left my dressing gown up at the pool. I made my way round to the Witch's Finger, which stood leaning over majestically in front of the Art Room, pointing towards the valley beyond.

What I saw there fair took my breath away. A nun was digging frantically in the earth, her breath ragged, a tiny sliver of moonlight catching on the enormous metal spade she was wielding. I knew that person – and I had thought she was on our side! Suddenly everything I thought I knew shifted, and I felt weird and strange, like I did when I fainted in Chapel. I was falling, falling backwards...wait! What was going on? A strong pair of arms supported me, breaking my fall.

Chapter 8

A mysterious disappearance

"Tom!" I said, when I came round.

"Shh!" he said. "And it's Father Tom to you."

I tried to explain how I'd decided to call both him and Anne by their names now, without the silly title of Father and Sister, but he shushed me again, then pointed ahead to the figure digging beneath the Witch's Finger.

"Tell me later," he whispered. "At the moment, I'm trying to work out what on earth my aunt, Sister Ignatius, is doing with that spade. For the life of me, I can't think of any explanation that would make sense."

"Don't you mean what *in* earth," I said with a giggle, adding, "instead of what *on* earth – she's digging *in* the earth, right?"

Tom sighed. "You're a very clever girl, Trixie," he said, "but sometimes I forget how young you are. I suppose that seems funny to you, but quite frankly...hang on, she's sitting down now."

"She's crying," I observed.

I hadn't known nuns could cry. It seemed weird. Like when one of the sixth form had seen Sister

Edward in Marks and Spencer's underwear department buying a bra and of course the news had spread like wildfire through the whole school with many exclamations of,

"What? Are you kidding?"

"A bra? You must be joking."

"Nuns wear modern underwear?"

"Do they have to buy it for themselves, I mean actually go to the shops?"

"How do they have any money?"

"Did the bra have lace on?"

"Shouldn't they have to buy stuff in the sale?"

"Was it a white bra? Or do they have to wear black, like their habits?"

"A black bra? That's not suitable..."

"Trixie!" Tom said, shaking me. "Have you fainted again? Take a deep breath or something. I'm going over, to see what the matter is."

Sister Ignatius was lying full length on the ground now, beating the earth with her fists.

"I can't remember where I buried it," she sobbed as Tom put his hand on her arm. "It was around here somewhere, but it all looks the same at night and the soil's so hard and full of tree roots."

Tom scooped her up and laid her beside me.

"From the beginning," he commanded. "What did you bury?"

Sister Ignatius wiped her tears away and looked at me in surprise. "Trixie! What are you doing here?"

Tom held his hand up. "No time for that. Just tell

me what you were looking for."

"Why, the Elizabethan treasure belonging to our foundress, of course – St Hilda, of the famous Poyntz family. You know the history, how she established our order of nuns..."

"Yes, yes," Tom said, "but to the point. You mean you buried treasure here? Why?"

"I got scared when Sister Anne said she'd seen mysterious strangers on our property – I began to think how easy it would be for unwelcome visitors to steal our ancient riches. We need these valuables for use in times of emergency, for example if it ever became necessary to save the school. There's enough wealth in those jewels to keep the school going in perpetuity."

It was on the tip of my tongue to ask why Sister Ignatius hadn't thought to just lodge the stuff in a bank vault if it was worth that much. Digging holes on the hillside and stuffing things into them at the dead of night seemed a rather strange way to protect an inheritance, but I knew how unworldly the nuns were and reckoned she thought she was doing her best.

"Let's have another look," Tom suggested and picked up the abandoned spade.

He dug vigorously for some time, then cried out in triumph, "Oh, is this what you were looking for?"

He held aloft a wooden padlocked box.

"The Lord has heard my prayers," Sister Ignatius said. "Praise be!"

Tom wiped his brow. It would have been nice if some of the praise heaped on the Almighty could have come his way, wouldn't it?

Sister Ignatius fished inside the neck of her habit and whipped out a key on a piece of string; she opened the creaking lid of the ancient box to reveal a very fancy and sparkly set of rubies and emeralds set in gold, in a heavy ornate Elizabethan style.

"The Poyntz family jewels," she murmured. "Left to the nuns by St Hilda and usually stored…"

"Don't tell me where you usually keep them," Tom said. "Just get them back there and be grateful we managed to find them again before someone else did. Although to be honest, I don't think that is what any possible intruders were after. I think there's something else."

Or someone else. A strange suspicion took root in my mind – then flew out again.

"We should talk to Sister Anne," Sister Ignatius said. "See if she's remembered any more details about the strangers she saw that led to this investigation in the first place."

Tom scratched his head. "Anne was meant to be here tonight. We had all planned to meet here and Trixie was going to tell us if she'd managed to find anything out. She's been for a midnight swim."

Sister Ignatius stared at me and started to mutter something about a detention, when I piped up, "It wasn't a midnight swim – we went earlier than midnight – and Sister Anne said there was no specific rule against swimming because the nuns hadn't thought anyone..."

"...would be so silly," Sister Ignatius finished. "Really Trixie, I'm surprised you would be that irresponsible..."

"But I have to tell you," I burst out, "oh, I should have told you straight away but what with fainting and then the jewels and so on...we were all terrified up there, at the swimming pool."

"I should think you were," Sister Ignatius said. "It could have been very dangerous."

"No," I shouted, "we were terrified because there was a man up there, with an Australian accent. First, we saw someone in the Laundry, then he must have followed us up to the pool."

"Who's the 'we'?" Sister Ignatius said. "How many of you were there?"

"At least half my form." I hung my head. With hindsight, it did seem a little reckless.

"Someone in the Laundry?" Tom said.

"Yes, but we thought at first it might be Sister Phoebe, that the other nuns were making her work really hard doing the laundry at night and we all resolved to keep our clothes as clean as we could so that she could have more time off..."

My voice trailed away as I saw the incredulity in Sister Ignatius' eyes and the bafflement in Tom's.

"Wait," he said, "an Australian accent?"

"That's right."

"And where is Sister Anne?" Sister Ignatius said.

"She sent me a note not long ago this evening,"

Tom said. "Pushed it under the door of Father Cuthbert's flat where I'm staying. I was a little surprised she didn't knock at the door and deliver the message in person, but it was quite late and she probably didn't want to disturb Father Cuthbert."

"What did the message say?" I asked.

"Only that she wouldn't be able to make it this evening – terrible headache – but that I should go ahead and meet you here and we could talk tomorrow."

I glanced at my watch. "It is tomorrow! It's one minute past midnight. Let's go to her room and talk to her."

The three of us hared off as fast as we could. We must have made an unlikely sight, Sister Ignatius in her full habit hitched up around her slim legs, highly polished lace-up shoes pounding across the grass, me in a nightie and tweed coat, and Tom striding out way ahead, calling out,

"Anne! Anne! My darling! Are you all right?"

"He's not calling her Sister Anne," Sister Ignatius said. "And he seems very fond of her."

"Yes," I agreed as I ran beside her. "They've got onto first name terms."

"Good thing too," Sister Ignatius said. "Not cut out to be a nun, that one – needs more excitement than a convent can provide. I'd hoped for something like this...of course, she's not taken her final vows, so it's not a problem...and we could have the wedding here, in the Chapel."

The speed of her imagination was seriously impressive – what a woman!

"Sister Ignatius," I asked, "was that why you asked Tom, I mean, Father Tom, to step in to investigate the sightings of the mysterious strangers, so that he would fall in love with Sister Anne and vice versa?"

Sister Ignatius smiled enigmatically, then tossed her head and muttered, "God works in mysterious ways, but sometimes needs a helping hand."

I already knew that nuns liked to interfere and plan other people's futures; they constantly talked to us either about taking the veil, or becoming wives and mothers, but I hadn't expected such direct intervention as this.

"I didn't take Sister Anne's sightings of the mysterious strangers very seriously," Sister Ignatius continued. "I mean, if there really were strangers on the premises, if you or any of the girls had been in danger, I should have called the local police, shouldn't I?"

"I don't know," I said. "I don't know much about these things." I wondered whether I should remind her I was only eleven, but she had a faraway look in her eyes and was rambling freely now.

"I thought it more probable that Sister Anne was mistaken about seeing strangers. She was at Drama College, you know, before she came to us. She's highly creative and talented. I'm sure you've heard the Irish accent she likes to put on, and we've all seen her limping and she does a good funny walk too, plus an excellent rendition of Lady Bracknell from *The Importance of Being Earnest*."

"I love Lady Bracknell! *A Handbag?*"

"Quite so! Anyway, even though I thought Sister Anne was probably mistaken about seeing strangers, nevertheless, I became anxious about the safety of our precious Poyntz treasure and buried it under the Witch's Finger one night last summer. There are some wicked people in the world, so I am told."

That made sense – sort of. As much as anything made sense at St Hilda's.

"Why did Sister Anne join the convent?" I asked.

"She said she'd had a sudden vocation, but if you ask me, it was something to do with a family situation. She comes from a very wealthy family."

"Like Hilda Poyntz, who founded the order?" I asked.

"Yes," Sister Ignatius said, "although that was over four hundred years ago. There was some odd situation over inheritance in Sister Anne's family and I think she just wanted to get away from it all. Her parents were killed in a tragic car accident, and when she comes of age, at 21, she'll be a rich heiress. But who cares about money?"

Well, for starters, Sister Ignatius did – otherwise she wouldn't have been so upset when she thought she had lost the Poyntz jewels.

I began to flag now; I couldn't see Tom at all – presumably he'd already gone into the main building to look for Anne in the Nuns' Quarters.

"Hurry!" Sister Ignatius said as she pulled me across the Nuns' Lawn; we went in through the door under the main staircase, meeting Tom as he ran down towards us, a stricken look on his face.

"She's gone!" he said. "Not in her room. Sister Edward's room is right next door to Anne's and she said she heard a scuffle and came out to see what was happening about an hour ago, then she herself got hit on the head by a ruffian and has only just regained consciousness. I've called the police. Anne must have been kidnapped – and the cowardly brute who took her presumably forced her to write the note to me saying she had a headache, then delivered it to Father Cuthbert's flat before he stole my darling Anne away."

Chapter 9

The police arrive

After that, all hellfire broke loose, if that isn't the wrong image to use in a convent. There seemed to be blue flashing lights everywhere as masses of police cars roared up the drive and inevitably the entire population of girls and nuns swarmed out of the front door in high excitement. There hadn't been an event like this ever before, in the whole history of the school.

"This is more exciting than when Mam'zelle forgot to come to teach the Upper 5s and we all went on a run across the fields instead."

"It beats the time we had that retreat and a young priest came to hear our confessions and we laughed so much we were nearly sick because he was *so* good looking."

"Yes, and do you remember when he said we could ask any question, any question at all? And that Spanish girl in the Lower Sixth stood up and asked him point blank, 'What should you do if you fall in love with a priest?'"

"Oh my, yes, I remember hearing that. Hey, was it actually true?"

"And did you know, apparently Sister Anne has fallen in love with Father Tom?"

"That can't be true."

"And he's not a real priest. See, over there – he's talking to the other policemen as if he's a policeman."

"He *is* a policeman; that's what Trixie told me."

"How does Trixie know these things?"

"Sister Anne's been kidnapped!"

"By aliens?"

"Don't be silly. But it's true, she's fallen in love with a priest, although he's not a priest, he's Sister Ignatius' nephew, so that's romantic, not forbidden love."

"But she's a nun!"

"Ah, but she isn't – yet – is she?"

"We all begged her only the other day not to take her final vows."

"We even sang 'Climb every Mountain' when we saw her in the corridor and she nearly tripped over, she was so surprised."

"Surprised? That you could sing?"

"No, silly! Surprised because we'd reminded her, in a very subtle way, that Julie Andrews was a nun in 'The Sound of Music' and she fell in love and it all turned out just fine."

"Apart from the family having to run away from the Nazis and so on..."

"Oh yes! I say, you don't think..."

"No, of course not! It's 1970. The war finished ages ago."

"If I could have your attention, ladies," a stern voice belonging to the most important looking policeman began.

We took absolutely no notice but carried on shrieking and chattering, our speculations and embroidering of pitifully few snippets of real information about Tom and Anne reaching feverish proportions.

"I heard they're secretly married already."

"And they spent their wedding night under the stars, with a silver bucket of chilled champagne and quantities of fresh strawberries in a picnic provided by the nuns – they allowed them to sit on the Nuns' Lawn, you know. We're never allowed on the Nuns' Lawn."

"Wasn't Sister Phoebe one of the bridesmaids?"

"Yes, almost definitely. Sister Edward sang a solo and Father Cuthbert performed the wedding ceremony in the Chapel in the dead of night."

"Just like Romeo and Juliet!"

"Hopefully not, as we all know what happened to them."

"Did you say Sister Anne is dead? Wait, she killed herself, thinking that Romeo, I mean Father Tom, was dead...we did that in English Lit last year."

"How tragic."

"Girls!" Sister Edward roared. Two hundred pairs of eyes rotated to stare at her and there was silence. At last.

"Ludicrous! Ridiculous! Totally untrue and

probably libellous! Yes, Father Tom is in real life a policeman and has been working undercover at St Hilda's. No one knew about this save Sister Ignatius and Sister Anne. Oh, and one of the New Bugs, ahem, new girls, Trixie. And yes, it's true that Sister Anne hasn't yet taken her final vows, but this does not, repeat, does *not* mean she has suddenly turned into Julie Andrews and is about to marry Tom – although now I come to think of it, that would be a happy outcome. However, the real problem is she's been kidnapped so it would be for the best if you all held your tongues and listened to what the Inspector has to say."

Two hundred necks then swivelled to face the most important looking man there.

"Inspector!" Sister Edward said. "The floor is yours."

The poor man was looking terrified by now, as well he might; he had obviously never encountered such a large gathering of schoolgirls and nuns in the middle of the night before and he turned quickly and fortified himself from a small hip flask before daring to face us again.

"Do you think that's got Communion Wine in?" Natalie said in a stage whisper that resonated eerily round the drive, bouncing off the high stone walls.

Sister Ignatius fixed her with a laser-like beam of disapproval, while Sister Edward mouthed "No!" and the Inspector was then free to make his speech.

"Inside," he yelled. "Inside all of you. Line up in the Hall in your forms and we'll interview you one by one to see if we can find out anything of interest."

Very soon we were all crammed into the Hall and the atmosphere relaxed. One at a time we were led out to the anteroom to 'have a chat' with the Inspector.

I was one of the first to be interviewed, at Tom's insistence, and I had to tell the Inspector all about what we had seen and heard at the Laundry and the swimming pool earlier in the evening. It all seemed so long ago now, but I tried to give a good account of what we had witnessed, without too much speculation or embellishment. I decided not to tell the Inspector about how Sister Ignatius had hoped that Tom and Anne might get married as it didn't seem the sort of information he was looking for, but I did tell him about the treasure and he seemed of the opinion that the sooner the nuns got the Poyntz jewels into a bank vault, the better.

When I went back into the Hall, I found that several girls had got bored waiting for their turn to talk and had produced jacks from their pockets and crouched on the floor to begin a tournament as if this were a normal Sunday afternoon, not the middle of the night after a kidnapping. Others had started dancing a Scottish reel and I thought I'd help by playing a Bach Minuet on the massive old grand piano in the corner, but the music wasn't really suitable and Sister Edward soon put a stop to the festivities. However, she said she understood we all felt we needed cheering up, so she was going to break the habit (excuse the pun) of a lifetime and let us have a look in the box of 'worthless' books that were usually given out at the beginning of the weekend and had to be given back by Sunday evening.

The nuns had a very weird attitude to reading in my opinion. When I was at home, my parents basically let me read anything I could find in the house, reasoning that if perhaps it was a little bit too old for me, I wouldn't understand it anyway, so no harm done.

The nuns, on the other hand, restricted the books we brought from home; I was still angry about my copy of *The Diary of Anne Frank* being confiscated as it had been considered somehow unsuitable for me, even though Sister Edward had taken pity and restored it to me on my first night. We were allowed to read books from the library of course, but only from the shelves deemed suitable for our age group. Then at weekends, we were allowed to read what they called 'worthless' books, which were adventure stories or light romances, maybe Mary Stewart, that sort of thing. Definitely no Jackie Collins or anything which might have had descriptions of unsuitable happenings, or events the nuns described as *physical* or *intimate*. You were allowed to borrow a 'worthless' book only for the weekend, giving it back on Sunday evening. If you hadn't finished it, which was highly probable, you still couldn't keep it and you couldn't reserve it for the next weekend either. There had been quite a lot of speculation about the probable endings to various worthless books, and I liked to think I had suggested some of the more imaginative possible dénouements.

"Here we are, girls," Sister Edward said as she dragged a vast cardboard box of books from a cupboard. "Take your pick."

"Wow!" Natalie said. "We're allowed to do some worthless reading."

"I'm half way through this one," Cath said, picking up a volume. "I'm going to find out what happened to the girl who ran away from home...I wonder if she discovered the secret of life after flying in a spaceship to Mars, like you suggested the plot might be, Trixie?"

Probably not. To be fair, that hadn't been one of my best suggestions.

"Where do all these books come from, Sister Edward?" I asked.

"Mostly confiscated when girls return from the holidays or an exeat weekend," she replied.

By now girls had homed in from all directions, eagerly reaching forward to pull books out of the box, then sitting cross-legged on the floor to devour them. I looked at the cover of the book I had chosen; a rose and a dagger were depicted, together with a cheerful looking couple holding hands.

"That's a good one, that is," Sister Edward muttered as she glanced at my choice. "Cracking plot."

I widened my eyes to Cath, who immediately started giggling. The giggling spread to Natalie, then to the girl next to her and across the group until we were all completely hysterical with mirth, with most of the group having no idea how or why they had joined in.

I bit my lip suddenly as I came back to earth with a jolt. What was I thinking of? How could I have forgotten poor Sister Anne? I wondered where she was now and how long it would be before we had some good news. Looking around, I saw that the police had all come into the Hall and the nuns were standing in a semi-circle looking serious.

"Girls!" Sister Ignatius' commanding voice rang out over the chuckling and chattering. "Girls! Could I have your attention? The police interviews have finished and you are all to go back to bed – yes, Natalie, you do have to put the worthless books back now. You are to say a special prayer for dear Sister Anne who I am sure is safe and well, and will be restored to us very soon, God be willing. There will be no talking on your way back to bed and you will be allowed an extra hour's sleep to make up for the events of the night. Chapel will therefore be at 8am tomorrow, so that you can have a lie in."

We were all feeling too tired and despondent to cheer this news, but stood up in silence and filed out of the Hall, making our way down the long corridors to our dormitories, questions buzzing through our minds.

What would tomorrow bring? Where was Sister Anne and how was she faring? Would Tom be able to rescue her, would they get married – and did two hundred bridesmaids seem too many?

Chapter 10

A message from Anne

The next morning I woke early, despite the events of the previous night, and picked up my copy of *War and Peace* from where I had hidden it under the bed. I hadn't dared risk leaving it out for Sister Edward to find, for if she'd thought *The Diary of Anne Frank* was unsuitable for an 11 year old, whatever would she have thought of *War and Peace*? I was keen to read a few more pages before I had to get dressed and go to Chapel. To my surprise, when I opened the front cover of the book, a note floated out; it disappeared under my bed and I was forced to grovel around in an undignified way to retrieve it.

"Morning!" the sixth former said as she flipped my curtain open. "Benedicamus...Oh, there you are! Lost something?"

I thought of saying oh no, I always start my day by crawling under the bed, but merely gave a sweet smile.

"Don't be late for Chapel!"

The curtain fell and I unfolded the paper with trembling fingers. I had already recognised Sister

Anne's stylish italic writing and was eager to read the contents.

Dear Trixie,

This is a 'just in case' note. Hopefully I will be with you soon – but maybe not, and so for that reason I have left you details of my suspicions and the facts, as far as I know them.

"Trixie?" Sister Edward growled, peering through my curtain. "Why aren't you dressed? What have you there?"

"Nothing," I lied, leaping up and trying to look busy with my clothes.

"Sister Edward," a voice came from the next cubicle. It was Natalie. "Sister Edward! Do we have to get up so early?"

"You've had a short lie in," Sister Edward said, going through to the next door cubicle. "I know you haven't had a full night's sleep, but you will have to manage. Offer it up."

I took the chance to scan through the rest of Anne's note as I hastily pulled my clothes on.

To find the full account, go to our arranged place, which for reasons of security I won't refer to here. I'm going to slip this piece of paper into your 'War and Peace' when I help you move your stuff from The Box back to the Cubicles tonight. I know how much you love the book so I feel sure it won't be long before you find...

"Line up!" Sister Edward commanded. "At the double!"

Botheration! How I missed being in The Box –

peace, quiet and the opportunity to read as much as I wanted. And to think, they only put me there as a punishment.

My mind was full of ideas of how to get banished there again as I made my way to the back of the crocodile, feet dragging, shoe laces undone. Maybe I could ask Sister Ignatius if she'd breakfasted on sour grapes? Or trip Sister Edward up? Organise another midnight swim?

The singing in Chapel this morning was on the muted side, with everyone exhausted, but for once I didn't feel faint. I was too busy trying to work out where Anne had hidden her next note. She said I'd know where it was – that we'd talked about it – of course! The Tower. I hadn't needed to go up there and put anything in the secret hiding space behind the stone yet, more's the pity, but that must be the place she'd meant. But when could I go and have a look? We were supervised from morn till night… unless I could sneak away during piano practice later in the day.

Suddenly I had a better idea – one that would not result in my missing out on the comforting melodies of Bach, always my solace.

"Cath," I said, nudging her as she stood beside me in the pew. "Cath! I feel faint."

"Shall I take you outside?"

"Yes, please."

She smiled at Sister Edward as I stumbled past the row of girls in our bench and I tried to look as drawn and unwell as possible, clutching at my stomach for good measure, making several girls lean back in alarm.

"Come straight back, Cath," Sister Edward whispered, "once Trixie is safely sitting on her chair outside."

Cath nodded. "Come on, Trixie; take my arm. There now..."

Once we were outside, I thought of admitting to Cath that it was merely a ruse, but I didn't want to involve her in my deception. Her parents still hadn't recovered from the shock of her sister being expelled and it would pain them greatly if Cath got into any sort of trouble.

"I'll be fine, Cath," I said. "I'm feeling a lot better, but I'll just sit here quietly for a bit."

Everyone was used to my fainting now and the nuns didn't follow me out of the Chapel anymore or even supply me with cups of tea, let alone a currant bun as they had done the first time I'd fainted. I was left to get on with it.

Soon I was on my own, head down between my knees, sitting on a squeaky wooden chair. I looked about carefully then raced off in the direction of the Hall.

Once there, I practically skied across the floor as my heel landed in a magnificently silky patch of beeswax polish on the ancient floorboards, coming to a halt at the door to the stone stairs that led to the Tower. I would have to be quick, as Chapel would be over soon and it was unthinkable that I would not be missed at breakfast. Sadly, there were quite a few cases of anorexia amongst the pupils, and as a result the nuns were fanatical about mealtimes and eating enough.

Racing up the steps, I grazed my knee on the rough stone wall in my hurry to climb the narrow staircase. Being late for breakfast wasn't my only motivation for hurrying; I had a hatred of being confined in small spaces and going up a long winding staircase was highly likely to provoke an asthma attack.

I found the loose stone at the top easily enough and pulled it out, coughing as a cloud of fine dust filled my lungs. Reaching deep inside the cavity and praying there wouldn't be a spider or worse waiting to pounce, I retrieved a thick crumpled envelope and stuffed it in my pocket. After replacing the stone, I fled the scene, coughing and spluttering.

"Who's there?" called a voice from below in the Boot Room as I stood at the bottom of the stairs, trying to catch my breath before running across the Hall. "Who's there? I am Sister Phoebe. I know there's someone there."

I stifled my coughs, resulting in a high pitched but mercifully softer wheezing emanating from my chest. It must be later than I had thought – Chapel had finished and I should be in the Refectory by now.

"If you're an angel, God bless you!" she called. "But if you're the devil, be away with you!"

Sister Phoebe was a simple and holy soul, much

loved by the whole community. I decided to risk an answer.

"It's an angel, sent by God to say he is well pleased with you and you needn't worry about a thing."

This sounded unconvincing, even to my ears.

There was a silence, then I could hear Sister Phoebe's feet starting to come up the stairs from the Boot Room.

"I know it's you, Trixie, my child," she said. "I recognise your wheezing."

Cripes! What was I going to do now?

She stood in front of me. "I'm sorry for your disorders, for your breathing and your fainting. It must be hard."

Not at all what I'd expected.

"I, I'm not in trouble?" I asked.

She laughed. "In trouble? Not with me, my child. Now run along."

I inflated my lungs for the mad run I was about to undertake to the Refectory and the rasping wheeze echoed on the stone stairs.

"But if you are ever in trouble, my child," she called after me, "I'm here for you. Don't you forget it."

As I alternately ran and stumbled along the corridors, gasping slightly, I felt a warm glow. I had an ally – Sister Phoebe. And Cath was my friend. Some of the other girls were softening towards me too, since we'd been on the midnight swim. Even Natalie had smiled at me this morning, which was unheard of.

As I rounded the corner to complete the last lap of the journey into the Refectory, I patted Anne's letter in my pocket. Perhaps I shouldn't take it into breakfast? The nuns had been known to make girls turn their pockets out before now, to check for pieces of bread or fruit being smuggled out of the Refectory. It wouldn't do if they found this, particularly before I'd had a chance to read it.

I took a quick detour and ran to the Cubicles, hiding Anne's words inside *War and Peace* with her first note. Now I just had to work out how to find the time to read it later.

Soon I was standing in the breakfast line in the Refectory, holding a plate. It was a fry up. Again.

I tried valiantly to look grateful when a shiny pitted fried slice of Mother's Shame oozing with grease was plonked onto my plate, followed by two fatty gristly sausages, black at one end and pink the other, plus a dollop of beans.

"Tomato?" the serving nun asked.

I nodded, waiting for my breathing to return to normal. Sister Edward strode past the queue then came to an abrupt halt when she saw me.

"Conduct mark, Trixie!" she barked. "You were late to breakfast – with no permission or excuse."

She hadn't actually checked whether I'd had either, but I shrugged my shoulders and managed to make the required response with a bowed head.

"Sorry, Sister Edward."

"Go and sit down. Eat. And no talking, as a punishment."

Was the no talking instead of the conduct mark or as well as it? Best not to ask. Besides, if Sister Edward only knew what other crimes I'd already committed this morning, she'd have given me several detentions, for sure.

I flopped down at my table, next to Cath. One of the nuns was already clearing the other side of our table, dabbing at some crumbs with a damp blue and white Jay cloth which she then popped back into an empty plastic margarine tub before she scampered off elsewhere to look for some more mess to deal with.

"Does your mother keep a Jay cloth in a margarine tub?" I asked Cath. "It seems bonkers to me, but all the nuns do it."

Cath laughed. "My mother doesn't even own a Jay cloth," she said.

"But what does she use to wipe the kitchen surfaces at home?"

"She knits her own dishcloths." Cath scraped her chair back, ready to take her plate up to the trolley to be stacked. "She knits everything."

I grinned. Cath had already told me about her home life. Her parents lived in remote Welsh countryside – they'd 'dropped out' and were living the good life, which seemed to consist of keeping chickens, knitting and making pottery mugs. All only possible, of course, because Cath's father had worked for years in a highly paid job in a firm of city lawyers. They'd tried sending Cath to the local school near their small holding in Wales, but it wasn't very local at all and she'd had to travel miles and miles every day on the bus, so they'd sent her to St Hilda's, despite the fact that her sister's scholastic career had not been successful and she'd been expelled. Rumour was they'd had to beg the nuns to take Cath and promise she would behave better than her sister, but I reckoned the nuns had secretly been glad to get another pupil and had only made a fuss because it was expected.

Cath was shaping up to be a really good friend, and it was high time I told her about all the business with Anne and Tom.

I stuffed the last piece of fried bread into my mouth and washed it down with lukewarm tea. Maybe I would tell her everything later once I'd read the letter from Anne in my piano practice time this afternoon, the first time for the whole day I would be by myself and able to do anything unobserved. It struck me then that this must be what prison would be like. Constant supervision, institutional food and grumpy jailers.

"Hurry up, Trixie!" Sister Edward screeched when she noticed me sitting there. "You haven't got all day. Get a move on!"

I comforted myself with the fact that not all the jailors seemed against me – Sister Phoebe's kind words still spread over me like a warm blanket of hope.

I jumped to my feet, and immediately the nun with the margarine box and Jay cloth sprang into action, sweeping away every trace of my meal from the table. On the other side of the Refectory, various girls who'd been caught shouting or generally misbehaving were stacking chairs on the tables, while another nun whizzed round gathering food debris from under the tables with her broom. That's Brum, not Brooom, of course.

The level of cleanliness in the convent amazed me – another strange and unexpected aspect of everyday life. Every single surface was kept gleaming with daily attention from the nuns. Hopefully I would be able to attempt a similarly efficient clean-up operation and sweep away the murky mystery that had resulted in Anne's disappearance.

Newly invigorated, I charged along the corridor to the Cubicles to make my bed and submit to a tidiness inspection, crossing my fingers as I remembered I'd shoved a load of belongings into my cupboard. Please, let it be 'under the bed and chest of drawer inspection' this morning, not 'cupboard inspection'. I couldn't afford to get another order mark. Or was it a conduct mark? No, order marks were for things kept in order, like your shoes being clean and your cupboard being tidy, but conduct marks were to do with how you behaved, the way you conducted yourself. I sighed; I had found it very easy to run up vast amounts of both conduct and order marks so far this week and the day of reckoning would soon be here. At the beginning of every week in Assembly, the nuns read out not only your academic marks and place in class, but also the total of your order marks and conduct marks. I screwed up my face, trying to remember what day it was. Lack of sleep and excitement over the whole kidnap business had addled my brain.

"Trixie!" Sister Edward was behind me in the corridor now. "Will you hurry up? You should be in the Cubicles by now for inspection. Then it's double quick to the Hall for Assembly. It's Monday morning! Everyone's marks will be read out to the whole school."

I bit my tongue to stop myself blurting out that I couldn't give a damn, then I suddenly remembered with joy that my place in class was first, so I would be leading my class into the Hall. I had actually come first in the class for academic work, in only my second week at St Hilda's! I had found this out last Friday, when we'd crowded round the noticeboard in the form room as we had at the end of the first week when I'd come last, but with everything that had gone on over the weekend, it had completely slipped my mind. Surely the nuns would be pleased with me, to know that I'd fulfilled my potential? I ran as fast as I could back to my cubicle, blotting out Sister Edward's enraged roar,

"Trixie! I said no running!"

Chapter 11

Confiscation

"Without self-discipline, Trixie, your life will not amount to anything. Girls? What does Trixie need to develop?"

"Self-discipline," everyone chanted back to Sister Ignatius.

My cheeks flamed as I stood in front of the entire school in Assembly for ritual humiliation. I should have been leading my class into their positions this morning as I'd come first for academic work; I'd felt happier and more full of purpose in my second week and had finally managed to concentrate enough in lessons to tackle the work. Sitting nearer the front of the class had helped too, because I could read the board properly. However, Sister Ignatius had decided that I was not to be afforded the great privilege of standing at the top of the line, in fact even my position of first in the form was to be erased forever from the record. I had gathered so many conduct and order marks in the past week that Sister Ignatius had it in mind to award me an Olympic Medal for Poor Behaviour and another for Untidiness and Deceit. She said I'd been lucky not to be sent back to be imprisoned in The Box again.

I think what had tipped me over the edge into total disgrace had been Sister Edward's discovery of the tangle of unwashed clothes, books and bits of paper heaped up in my cupboard in the Cubicles this morning; I had committed the serious error of shoving all my mess in the cupboard, thinking it was an 'under the bed and chest of drawers inspection day' instead of what it was in reality – the 'cupboard inspection day'.

I hung my head as Sister Ignatius catalogued my crimes to her rapt audience, Sister Edward taking over when she had to pause for breath.

"And so, girls," Sister Edward's voice rose in triumph, "Trixie's possessions, including some of her personal letters, will be confiscated until the end of next week."

"Indeed, they will!" Sister Ignatius folded her arms under her black cape and her eyebrows shot up until they touched her wimple. "Furthermore, she will have to prove she can behave before they are restored to her..."

Sister Edward stepped forward to interrupt at this point. "Although, I have to say, one of the books – *War and Peace* – will not be returned as that is a Sixth Form book, not suitable for a girl in the Lower 4. Trixie can only have got hold of that tome by some very underhand means..."

A collective gasp of horror ran round the room; I noticed sympathetic glances too, as well as bafflement – why would anyone want to read a book like that, anyway?

Sister Edward produced a cardboard box with my belongings in and, in a highly dramatic gesture, produced the key to the confiscation cupboard from a fold of her habit and locked the offending articles away in full view of the entire community.

I felt sick as I realised the copy of *War and Peace*, plus not only my first note from Anne but also her longer letter, were among those items. What was I going to do now? At least I knew the nuns hadn't read them, at least not yet, as there simply wouldn't have been time.

Eventually the Assembly turned to other matters and we all said some prayers about forgiveness and sang a song about what a wonderful world we lived in and how grateful we should be.

As I made my way out of the Hall at the back of my class line, where it seemed I was destined to remain forever, Sister Phoebe barged into me.

"Sorry my child! I am so clumsy." She then gave me the most enormous wink. "Come to the Laundry at break for some extra clothes, in case too many of yours have been confiscated."

I nodded my agreement and she beetled away.

Break time found me forgoing the pleasure of haring along the corridors with Cath. I made my excuses and hastened off to the Laundry, where Sister Phoebe was waiting for me – with my letter from the Tower, from Anne!

"How did you, why did you..." My voice trailed off as Sister Phoebe enveloped me in a warm hug, the first I'd had since arriving at the convent over two weeks ago.

"Sometimes you don't need to know how things happen; just take your letter. You can read it here if you want. Would you like some tea? And a Garibaldi?"

I sipped the lukewarm tea gratefully, feeling very grown up as we usually had water to drink at break. Once I'd devoured the squashed fly biscuit, a welcome but slightly stale treat, I turned my attention to Anne's letter.

"Shall I read it out loud," I asked, "or have you read it?"

"Read it out, please." Sister Phoebe settled back in a tiny armchair next to a humming washing machine.

I knew Sister Phoebe wouldn't have read my private correspondence. Sister Edward might have, but...

"I only didn't read it because I can't," Sister Phoebe confessed.

"Can't?"

"I can't read."

My mouth formed a perfect 'O' shape of astonishment. So, it was true! Natalie had mentioned in a sneering sort of way something about Sister Phoebe being illiterate, or, as she put it, 'a litter rat', but I'd never thought it could be true. I mean, in 1970, surely all nuns could read? But probably not nuns who might have come from a tiny rural community, a smaller more adult voice said from deep inside my head.

"Here goes," I said, picking up the letter.

Dear Trixie, I'll be as brief as I can but bear with me because I have to fill you in with a few details of my life before I joined the order and became a novice...

"She's not suited to the order," Sister Phoebe interrupted. "Not that one."

"Sister Ignatius said that the other day," I remarked.

"She's right," Sister Phoebe said. "When Sister Anne came to me to try on her habit – I make all the habits, by the way – she twirled around in it and looked disappointed."

"Disappointed? But you sew so beautifully," I said indignantly.

Sister Phoebe laughed then, a real belly laugh, chortling until the tears ran down her face.

"Bless you, child," she said finally when she could catch her breath. "Sister Anne wasn't intending to criticise my sewing."

"What was it then?"

"She said..." Sister Phoebe started off again now, holding her sides and rolling around on her chair.

"She said that the colour didn't suit her. Black wasn't her colour at all. Said she'd been reading in a magazine about how everyone fits into a different part of the wheel of colour, whatever that is, and her place in the circle was full of bright clear colours and she should never wear black. I told her then that if she felt things like that mattered, perhaps she shouldn't join us in our community – it wasn't that we didn't want her though, she shouldn't think that, I was just thinking about the best course of action for her personally. My goodness, we were thrilled to have a new recruit. We hardly have any novices now and there needs to be fresh blood every few years, otherwise who's going to look after all the ancient nuns?"

Sister Phoebe fixed me with a beady eye.

"Don't suppose you've ever thought of joining up, Trixie?"

I recoiled in horror, covering my face with my hands.

"Don't worry," she cackled, "that was in the way of a joke. Can't you tell? You're no more suited to the convent life than Anne."

I breathed deeply. Thank goodness for that! Life as a nun was not something I could see myself settling into, no way...

"So," Sister Phoebe continued, "carry on reading, my child."

I looked at the paper again and put on a grown up voice to read Sister Anne's words.

I was born into a wealthy family, and spent a happy childhood with my parents on their country estate. Sadly, they were not blessed with more than one child, so I was not fortunate enough to have siblings, but my father had a distant cousin, Philip, he used to spend time with as a boy. They fell out in later years – I'm not sure why...

"Heavens!" I looked at my watch. "I should be at my next lesson – must run!"

"Take these," Sister Phoebe urged, popping a few squashed fly biscuits into my hands. "You can visit me later and let me know what the rest says. Deal?"

I grinned, liking this remarkable lady more and more with every passing minute spent in her company.

"Deal!" I yelled and we shook hands before I rushed away, the letter tucked once again into my pocket. I was determined not to let it get confiscated again, so resisted the temptation to look at it in the rather tedious lessons we were forced to endure for the rest of the day.

French was the worst – I nearly exploded with sheer frustration when someone put their hand up to ask, "May we turn the page?"

Mam'zelle answered, quite seriously, "If you are sure you have written on the very bottom line, then yes, you may turn the page."

Could no one think for themselves?

"Are you all right, Trixie?" the French teacher asked. "You seem to be groaning."

"Yes," I managed to say. "Absolutely fine, Mam'zelle. Just struggling with a decision here; should I underline with one or two lines?"

An electric shock ran through the classroom as a few of the brighter characters realised I was being facetious, a bad fault of mine which Sister Edward pointed out constantly, but luckily Mam'zelle was of a trusting nature and, after considering carefully, said,

"I think you may decide that for yourself this time. I won't take any marks off whether you use single or double underlining."

"Oh goodie," Natalie said and a few of her friends who had been looking anxious for a moment were able to relax, clearly having been concerned about their grades.

I sniggered, quickly covering it with a cough, then was nearly undone when Cath looked at me cross-eyed and a terrible hysteria rose in me, resulting in a sudden fit of choking.

"Water," Mam'zelle said. "Trixie – you may go and get yourself some water."

"Thank you," I croaked as I leapt out of my seat and hurtled towards the door.

Once down in the cloakroom, I turned the tap on and managed to read a few more lines of Anne's note.

Philip had been a little unkind to my father I think when they were boys; this was just a suspicion, mind you, strengthened by the fact that when I was a teenager, Cousin Philip started writing regularly to my father from Australia – he had emigrated some years before – and my father seemed pleased and said it was time to build bridges.

When I was but eighteen, a terrible tragedy struck – both my parents were...

"Trixie!" Sister Edward roared. "Why are you here and why is that tap running? What a waste! Think of the unfortunate people abroad in underdeveloped countries with no fresh water."

"Mam'zelle sent me to get myself a drink of water. Frog in my throat in the, er, in the French lesson." I hid the letter behind my back and coughed a few times. "Bad cough developing."

"That does sound bad," Sister Edward conceded, adding, "Get back to class as soon as you can," before turning on her heel and striding off through the outside door. Her habit was pinned up on one side; she was obviously about to drive the lawnmower, one of her favourite tasks.

...*killed in a car accident*, I read.

Sister Ignatius had mentioned this to me before, but hearing about it from Anne herself made a deep impression on me. Tears sprang to my eyes as I rushed back to class, thinking how much Anne must have suffered. Was that what had encouraged her to take the veil?

Chapter 12

Anne's past

After an interminable afternoon, I finally read the rest of the letter when I was supposed to have been practising the piano and found that Anne's parents had been tragically killed when they had been staying with her father's distant Cousin Philip out in Oz.

Cousin Philip was marvellous at first, taking care of all the funeral preparations. I was only eighteen and had very little idea of what to do. He suggested the service should be held in Australia and so I flew out for the ceremony...it was right in the middle of my A levels, so I could only stay for a few days. During that time, I started to rely on Cousin Philip; he wanted to help me sort out financial matters amongst other things. I had no idea how much I was due to inherit when I turned 21 and he said he could help me manage the responsibility, if that would help; I only had to say the word and he would take control of everything. This didn't seem quite right, but I was grateful for his offer, as I thought it meant he cared.

Philip said it didn't matter if I didn't finish my A levels as I would be a rich heiress when I came of age, but I wanted to get back to England to finish my exams. I had a dream for further study too, to go to Drama College, which is what I did that autumn.

Philip visited me in England a few times and then everything went wrong and turned ugly. I don't know how it happened, but he got the idea in his head that we should marry. He said it had been my parents' dearest wish to unite the two distant sides of the family – and he declared himself to be madly in love with me.

There was so much wrong with this. He was far too old, I didn't love him and besides, he was a relative, even if a very distant one. Moreover, I began to suspect his motives were mercenary; I had found out that he had been jealous of the money my father had always enjoyed and felt that some of it should have been his by right, as part of a remote branch of the family. Anyway, the whole thing troubled me so much that for a while I became lost and confused, unsure of what to do for the best. I moved student digs several times and tried to cut all contact with Philip, but he stayed in England and seemed to have a knack for finding me.

In desperation I convinced myself I had a vocation to be a nun. I reckoned that the money I was due to inherit was the root cause of all the trouble and so I decided I would abandon my drama course, enter the convent and gift the whole inheritance to St Hilda's when I came of age. The nuns deserved my fortune more than Philip. And in the future, when I took my final vows and became a full nun, he would at last have to accept I would never marry him. Perhaps then he'd leave me alone for good.

What I didn't reckon with, Trixie dear, is that you can't enter a convent just to escape the world – you have to have a proper vocation. I was running away from a situation I couldn't deal with, instead of facing it. Perhaps I should have gone to the police or a lawyer or something, but I was too naïve and Philip had this knack of making me feel very small...

I left my parents' estate in trusted hands – they'd had very good staff to rely on – and then took the veil as a novice at St Hilda's. As time passed, all seemed well, and I didn't hear anything from Philip again, save an angry bitter letter saying I would regret my choice and he hoped I would be very unhappy as a nun. Throwing my life away, I think he referred to it as.

Then, last summer, I thought I saw a stranger down in the woods, on the other side of the Nuns' Lawn. It wasn't Philip, I was sure of that, but it unsettled me nonetheless. There were a few other times too when I felt as if I was being watched; I was concerned that Philip was renewing his efforts to gain control of my inheritance and that worried me terribly. If he wanted to persuade me, or, heaven forbid, force me into anything, he only had until December this year because that's when I will turn 21 and can do whatever I want with the money. When I told Sister Ignatius about seeing strangers on the school premises, I suspected she thought I had an over-active imagination, but even so, she called in her nephew, Tom, a policeman pretending to be a priest as you so cleverly guessed almost from the very beginning.

Please, dear Trixie, do something for me now; go to Sister Ignatius and show her this letter, Tom too. It's high time they both knew the full story of Philip and why I decided to become a nun.

I fear it won't be long before Philip makes another move; I am more convinced than ever that he is up to no good and I need to leave a record of my suspicions in case anything happens to me...

I let out a long, low whistle, understanding at last why Anne had been snatched. What an unspeakably vile man Philip was! I clenched my fingers into fists and decided then and there I would do everything in my power to help her. It was bad enough to have lost her parents in a tragic accident, but then to be betrayed by the one remaining family member who should have been there to protect and help her, why, it fairly made my blood boil.

"Don't you worry, Anne," I vowed. "We'll find you and get justice."

My hands grabbed at the piano keys and played a few fierce chords before I folded the letter up again and made my way to find Sister Ignatius and Tom.

They were both shocked beyond belief.

"The poor girl!" Sister Ignatius said.

"She's in real danger." Tom bared his teeth.

"Trixie!" Sister Ignatius said. "Why didn't you bring this to us earlier? You've had the whole day to do something."

I tried to explain how it had been difficult because the letter had been lost to me for a while, then later, I hadn't had much time to read it, what with lessons and so on...but I could see in their eyes I'd behaved foolishly by not going to them straight away, immediately after I'd made my discovery in the Tower that very morning. I felt embarrassed as I saw myself through their eyes – just a silly child. A large tear rolled down my cheek.

"I'm so sorry. I've let you and Sister Anne down."

"You did your best, Trixie," Tom said.

"Well," Sister Ignatius said, "I suppose if Anne hadn't trusted you, none of this information would have come to us, so we should be grateful for that."

I thought that was very generous of Sister Ignatius under the circumstances and I began to feel a little better.

"I've just thought," I began, "shall I, I mean, may I be excused? It's Sister Phoebe, you see. I have to let her know what the rest of the letter said."

My voice trailed off. Oh dear! I think I'd just got myself into hot water again.

"Sister Phoebe?" Sister Ignatius frowned. "And what has she to do with this?"

I was then compelled to share the details of how Sister Phoebe had taken the letter out of the confiscation cupboard that morning and had given me squashed fly biscuits and weak tea at break.

Tom put his hand on Sister Ignatius' arm as her eyes started flashing and her brows wriggled like demented insects.

"Aunt! Trixie really has done her best and so has Sister Phoebe. Sometimes...sometimes..."

"Sometimes the rules here stop us pupils being open and being able to jolly well get on with things!" I yelled.

Out of the three of us, I think I was the most surprised by my outburst. To my utter amazement, Sister Ignatius recovered first and said,

"Of course, you're right, Trixie. And Tom you're right too. Everyone is trying their hardest and doing their best and we need to work together as a team. No, you run along, Trixie, and tell Sister Phoebe all about it while Tom and I pass this on to the officer in charge of the investigation. I think your input has been most valuable. You may have, should have a mark of some kind..."

Her voice trailed off as she had to face the fact that the system of marks at St Hilda's only allowed for Conduct Marks or Order Marks, and they were exclusively for *bad* behaviour. There were marks for academic work of course, but nothing to reward good behaviour. Perhaps there wasn't anything we did the nuns thought was good, or perhaps they assumed good behaviour should be the default position and thus didn't need rewarding. Heaven forbid we should become too pleased with ourselves, big-headed or proud – after all, Pride was a sin, one of the more Deadly ones.

"There is much to think about," Sister Ignatius muttered as I hared off.

"Trixie!" Way in the distance, at the end of the corridor, Sister Edward had spied me. "Stop running! Take a conduct mark!"

I could just see her taking her small black book out of the folds of her habit as I smartly reversed back down the corridor and chose a different route to race along to the Laundry to see Sister Phoebe.

On the way there, I met Cath, and quite a few other girls too.

"Where are you off to?" Cath asked.

"Yeah," Natalie said. "Seem in a bit of a hurry."

Sister Ignatius had said I could tell Sister Phoebe all about what had happened but she hadn't said anything about not telling anyone else, so I shared a few choice titbits of gossip and invited the ever-growing group of girls to join me on my journey to the Laundry.

By the time I arrived, I felt like the Pied Piper of Hamlin, with an immense gaggle of shrieking happy faces following behind me. We all thronged into the Laundry, with some girls sitting on the floor and others perched together on chairs or standing squashed against the walls. If there had been chandeliers, there would have been girls swinging from them – it was that crowded.

Even though Anne's story was quite sensational enough, I manged to embroider it, adding fanciful details about her Cousin Philip's probable unpleasant appearance and character to make them shudder.

"He's probably mad!" Cath said.

"And he wants to marry her? Yuk!" Natalie grimaced at the thought.

Sister Phoebe passed round squashed fly biscuits and custard creams and for that short time, I was the most popular girl in the school, right at the centre of an amazing occasion.

But after a while, we sobered up and became anxious for Anne, some girls sobbing uncontrollably.

"What are the police doing?"

"Why haven't they found her yet?"

"Where do you think she is?"

"Will she be all right?"

Suddenly we realised it was supper time and we should have been in the Refectory five minutes ago. The Angelus bell rang out as we ran across the Quad and back into the main building, Sister Phoebe's voice calling out after us,

"Don't forget, girls! Get your rosary beads out tonight and pray for Sister Anne's safe return."

The noise in the Refectory was deafening as girls passed on the story of Sister Anne's evil distant Cousin Philip.

"Girls!" Sister Edward screamed. "Stop shouting! It's time for Grace. Time to give thanks."

I gave a silent prayer then to the Almighty, that he would look after Anne and bring her back to us safe and sound. I sent up another prayer too, that some of my sudden popularity might last, and that Natalie and her followers might get fed up with teasing me once and for all.

Chapter 13

Assembly

The highlight of our mornings was swarming around the carved shelf over the huge intricately decorated radiator in the Hall before Assembly began, waiting for our letters. We lived for The Post. So far, I had heard twice from my parents, cheerful missives all about their move to sunnier climes, but not so upbeat that I felt they weren't missing me. This morning, however, I was surprised to get a letter from my aunt. She lived in Devon and I was due to stay with her for half-term.

Your uncle and I are spending a week in the Lakes, leaving tonight, she wrote. *It's so beautiful up there with the wonderful colours, like a little slice of heaven...we'll be staying in a fabulous hotel, with the best food, so welcoming...*

Hmm. My aunt was not following the strict protocol of sending cheerful news, but not so cheerful that the person receiving it didn't feel a little put out that they were locked away in a boarding school. My heart sank even further to read about the beautiful walks she and my uncle were planning, the luxurious swimming pool at the hotel, and the amazing cream teas they were looking forward to tucking into.

I scuffed the toe of my shoe on the bare floorboards.

"Trixie!" Sister Edward appeared from nowhere. "You will have to polish out that mark on your shoe this evening in the Boot Room."

Before long, the entire school was standing in form rows, answering to our names as the school roll was called by the Head Girl. I had to hand it to her, she had this down to a fine art. Reading out over two hundred names without mispronouncing or stumbling was pretty amazing. But then, most of the school thought the Head Girl was pretty amazing. Standing in front of us in her impeccable uniform – no scuffed shoes for her – her waist-length blonde silky hair tied neatly back, she was an impressive presence. She even remembered to roll the 'r's of the Spanish pupils' names. When she had finished, she stepped aside to let Sister Ignatius address us.

"Girls!" We stood up even straighter. "I have to tell you some news this morning about Father Tom. He has left us for the time being, as he is helping the police with their enquiries into Sister Anne's sudden disappearance."

This wasn't exactly true – he might have been helping the police but that was because he was the police, or at least part of the police force. Sister Ignatius seemed to have forgotten that every single girl in the school knew that anyway, so

114

she needn't have been coy about revealing that he wasn't a priest. Everyone also knew that he was her nephew, indeed the talk after lights out since Anne had been kidnapped had covered this subject very thoroughly indeed. And we fully realised that Anne hadn't 'disappeared': she'd been kidnapped.

"Father Cuthbert will manage perfectly well without him, and no girl, I repeat, *no girl* under any circumstances, is to mention any of this to their parents when they write home this Sunday. The school telephone is out of action at the moment, so you won't be tempted to mention it during a call either."

Sister Ignatius beckoned me out of my line as I left the Hall and took me to a quiet corner of the Ante Room.

"You need to forget all about the mysterious goings on now, Trixie, and let the police take over. You've been very helpful in your own way, but the time has come to let the professionals deal with it."

She held a warning finger up as I drew breath to start protesting.

"No, Trixie. You have nothing to say on the matter. You need to focus on your studies now. And on developing self-discipline. You have a great deal of room for improvement."

As she swept off and I raced after my line of classmates, my heart sank. The excitement was over and I was to return to the dreary routine of everyday life.

I wondered vaguely if I should revert to my plan

of doing something really terrible so that I might be sent back to The Box; it would be fun to spend my time working my way through all the books in the library that were forbidden to me on account of only being eleven years old. However, on reflection, I thought I might as well stay in the Cubicles for a bit longer. Maybe Natalie and her chums would allow me to breathe more easily after the episode in the Laundry, and besides, Cath was turning into a really good friend and I'd miss her company if I went back to The Box.

As I reached the end of the corridor, Sister Edward appeared, blocking out the meagre autumn light.

"Trixie!" she boomed. "You are due at the opticians this morning. Your parents have asked for your eyesight to be tested after you did so appallingly in the first set of marks this term; they seem to think you might be unable to see the blackboard properly."

Sister Edward glared at me; somehow, I knew she thought this would turn out to be nonsense, merely an excuse for not Trying My Best.

"Go to the Ante Room and wait for a lift into town at morning break," she continued.

"Will I miss squash and biscuits?" I asked, devastated at the thought.

Sister Edward put her head on one side and a curious attempt at a smile spread over her features, then she reached into the folds of her habit.

"Here, take this," she said. "I believe you *will*

miss your break time snack and may have some need of sustenance. We can't have you fainting at the opticians, can we? They might think we don't know how to look after you."

I stared in amazement at the battered object partially wrapped in red shiny foil.

"It's called a Penguin," she said. "A Penguin Biscuit. See the little picture here, of the bird? I confiscated it last term and have been wondering what to do with it ever since. It's yours, if you want it."

"Thank you!" I stuffed the biscuit into my pocket and raced off to class, thrilled at the sudden act of kindness.

"Trixie!" Sister Edward screamed after me. "No running inside! Conduct mark!"

Chapter 14

A Trip To Town

I inspected my scuffed shoe as I waited in the Ante Room at morning break as instructed. Licking my finger, I rubbed the mark vigorously until it was much improved.

"There! Won't have to go the stupid Boot Room now," I muttered.

"Come along then," a voice said. "I'm ready to give you a lift into town."

"Sister Phoebe! I didn't know you were going to take me."

"I volunteered," she said. "I love driving and besides, I wanted to talk to you. I'm worried about Sister Anne. We need to do something."

Sister Phoebe put her fingers to her lips as there was a rustling sound behind us and Sister Edward prowled out of the Hall.

"Still here?" she rasped. "You'll be late if you don't get a move on."

We made our way outside to the nuns' ancient battered Mini; actually, I wasn't sure if it really was ancient, but it certainly looked it as it had suffered a vast number of minor prangs. Some girls said this was because Sister Phoebe was such a bad driver; I thought this very unfair. Granted, she struggled to see out of the windscreen on account of being so short, but I felt certain she was a skilled and sensible motorist.

Within minutes I realised how mistaken I had been. I clung to the side of the car, holding onto the door handle in sheer terror as Sister Phoebe roared down the drive before I had even fully closed my door.

"Watch out for the pot holes!" I screamed as I saw an enormous one looming. Too late. The car hit the side of the gigantic crater and jumped in the air, coming to land with a screech of tyres and the smell of burning rubber. Sister Phoebe's rosary beads, which were strung round the driver's mirror, swung from side to side as the car gathered speed again, racing past the majestic beech trees.

"Best to drive fast over the pot holes," Sister Phoebe said. "Then they're less of an obstacle."

Once we reached the end of the drive, she swung right into the main road; the oncoming traffic had to swerve to avoid her.

"Are you sure you're not the one who needs to visit the optician?" I asked.

"I know what the girls say about my driving – all grossly exaggerated. I love driving, used to drive tractors on my father's farm back in Ireland as a girl; there's nothing I'm afraid of on the road."

That may have been the case, but I still wished Sister Phoebe would slow down a little as I feared being stopped by the police. I pointed at the speedometer.

"Oh, don't worry about that," she laughed. "The police round here don't care about the rules; besides, they're all terribly friendly, great chaps, always fascinated by my rosary beads."

By some miracle, we got to the optician in one piece and Sister Phoebe clambered out of the Mini.

"See you later," she called, making her way down a side street.

"But Sister," I bleated. "Which way is it? Where is the optician? I've never been here before."

"Good heavens, child," she said, pointing across the road to a distant shop.

I screwed my eyes up and could just make out a sign with a pair of spectacles.

"I forgot you can't see properly," she giggled. "Here, take my arm; I'll help you across the road."

Traffic screeched to a halt as Sister Phoebe wandered into the road, hand held out like King Canute holding back the tide. One motorist stared until I thought his eyes would pop out of his head; I suppose he found it odd that a middle-aged lady dressed in a gentlewoman's costume from Elizabethan times, for that is what the nuns' habits were modelled on, had suddenly appeared in front of him in the middle of a road in 1970.

"Are you sure you don't want to come into the shop with me?" I asked Sister Phoebe.

"No, you'll be fine on your own," she replied. "Besides, I've got shopping to do. I need to stock up."

She rummaged in one of her Tardis-like pockets and produced a crocheted string bag which looked as if it dated back to the War.

"I made this thirty years ago," she announced. "Still in great condition and so useful."

"What sort of shopping?"

I didn't think nuns ever bought things, or even needed things. Hadn't they taken a vow of poverty and given up all their worldly goods?

"Supplies," she said. "Always useful."

I decided not to ask where she'd got the money from, not wanting to hear that she'd raided the confiscation cupboard again. Girls were forbidden to have money at school, but they often tried to smuggle it in at the beginning of term so that they could run down to the garage at the end of the drive on Sunday afternoons and buy sweets. The money was usually found and confiscated when we unpacked our trunks, but sometimes a lucky girl would manage to avoid this and complete the trek to the garage, returning with confectionery to share. If she was caught on her return, there was a letter sent home plus a Saturday detention to cope with, but most girls felt the excitement of sneaking down the drive combined with the wondrous taste of a contraband Mars Bar as they jogged back, pockets stuffed with other goodies for their friends, made it worth the risk.

The optician's door had a little bell which tinkled gently as I entered. I went to the counter and waited patiently for ages and ages, until a lady on the other side of the room said, "May I help?"

Ah, the reception desk was over there. I had been waiting by a stack of magazines on a table. Perhaps I really did need glasses?

"I've an appointment," I said. "For my eyes."

She glared at me. "You're late."

"Sorry," I mumbled.

"By one minute. But don't worry, the appointments are running late, so go and sit down."

I went back to the waiting area, picked up a magazine and enjoyed reading a fascinating article about how to pluck my eyebrows and then another about what to do with scrag end of lamb for an economical supper dish that all the family could enjoy.

Family. I blinked as I looked around, and felt a wave of homesickness. This was the first time I had been away from St Hilda's since the start of term.

"Hello! You must be Trixie."

A kind looking gentleman stood in front of me holding his hand out. "I see Sister Phoebe has left you to your own devices. Now, this way if you please..."

Very soon, I was reading out the names of letters while wearing a strange metal contraption into which the optician slipped glass lenses with a clicking sound.

"You're a little short sighted, that's all," he pronounced. "Nothing we can't deal with. You won't need to wear spectacles all the time, just in class or if you're watching a film, that sort of thing. Tell me, do you do a lot of reading? What's your favourite book?"

We spent a happy ten minutes discussing literature and then he said I'd probably find my eyes didn't get so tired when I had glasses and of course, it would be much easier to read things on the blackboard.

"Great news! I've had to sit right at the front of the class so that I could see the board. Now I won't have to!"

He laughed. "You'd rather sit at the back?"

"Much rather," I said. "It's safer at the back."

"Safer?"

"From Natalie and her friends," I explained. "They throw things at me when the teacher's not looking. It can be quite distracting, not to say painful. If I sit at the back, I can concentrate better and now I'll be able to see as well."

The optician frowned. "I might ring the school," he said, "if you don't mind."

"What about? Have I said something wrong? I'm often in trouble for saying the wrong thing. Sister Edward thinks I make facetious comments."

"Does she indeed?" the optician said, standing up. "Mmm...now, we need to choose some frames for you, young lady."

He took me over to a display in the main room. "These are the ones for children. One design, but you choose the colour – brown, pink or blue?"

I hesitated between the pink and the blue.

"Which do you think?" I asked.

The lady at the desk came over and she was smiling this time. "I think the blue," she said. "They'd go nicely with your eyes."

"Yes, I agree," the optician said. "And just a few measurements to take...that's it. You'll need to come back next week to collect your spectacles, and we will make sure they fit really well, maybe adjust them a little if needs be."

I clapped my hands together. "Another exeat!" I cried. "I can't believe how lucky I am, to escape from school twice!"

The optician and the receptionist looked at each other and then Sister Phoebe bounded through the door, her string bag bulging. If there had been a competition for the most packets of biscuits ever in a string bag, she would have won first prize.

"Time to go," she said and winked at me. "All done?"

"All done," the optician said. "Trixie's spectacles should be ready next week."

He held the door as Sister Phoebe and I crossed the road to the Mini. She flung her bag in the boot, then grabbed my arm.

"Let's be late back," she said. "We could go and take a peek at Gold Hill. I love Gold Hill!"

"Great!"

Soon we were standing at the top of one of the steepest streets in Britain.

"This was used in a film," Sister Phoebe said. "*Far From The Madding Crowd.*"

"Yes, I've seen that," I said. "In the cinema. It's really good. Not as sad as that other book by Hardy – you know, *Tess of the D'Urbervilles*."

I shouldn't have said that! Sister Phoebe couldn't read and so wouldn't know what I was talking about; to be helpful, I gabbled a quick précis of the plot, so she wouldn't feel left out.

"Poor Tess had a terrible time, didn't she?" Sister Phoebe said. "I hope they make that book into a film, because it could be quite colourful."

Sister Phoebe adored watching films but was limited to the ones that were shown to the school in the gym on the occasional Sunday afternoon.

"We need to work out how to find Sister Anne before anything like that happens to her." Sister Phoebe had a deep frown between her eyes.

I felt very alarmed then. "You surely don't think that Anne will be arrested at Stonehenge and hanged for murder like poor Tess?"

Sister Phoebe shook her head. "No, of course not. Because we're going to find her and rescue her before harm befalls her. You and me, Trixie, we need to be ready to spring into action. Meet me tonight after lights out in the Laundry and we'll hatch a plan to find Anne."

Chapter 15

Meeting in the Laundry

That evening I waited until everyone around me in the Cubicles was fast asleep, then slipped outside in my night clothes. As I stood on the muddy boot mat, I thought back to my first night at the school, only just over two weeks ago, when I'd been overcome with homesickness, desperately wanting to run back to my parents and leave the convent forever. I stepped forward and the metal mat rattled.

"Trixie!" It was Cath, on her way to the bathroom. "What are you doing? Are you going for a swim?"

"No, I'm going to see Sister Phoebe. I'll be back soon. Don't tell anyone."

"OK," she replied and pattered off down the corridor.

I shivered, then started to run to the Laundry, hoping the bats wouldn't be around tonight. Sister Phoebe greeted me with cocoa and the inevitable squashed fly biscuits.

"We need to do something," she said. "I'm fed up of waiting for news from the police and of not knowing how Anne is."

"I agree," I said, sipping my hot drink, "but what can we do? It's out of our hands now – Sister Ignatius said it was time to leave it to the professionals."

"Jolly good advice, in my opinion," a man's voice said from the shadows. "I say! Any more of that cocoa available? It's thirsty work rescuing damsels in distress. Squashed fly biscuit wouldn't hurt, either."

"Tom!" I said.

"And Anne!" Sister Phoebe shrieked. She flung her arms around Anne who was looking so different in ordinary clothes instead of her habit that I had trouble believing it was really her at first.

"How, what...?" I gasped.

"It's true," Anne said. "Tom rescued me! My Cousin Philip – he's really gone too far this time – had arranged for me to be kidnapped by one of the odious men who work for him..."

"Yes, yes," Sister Phoebe interrupted. "We know you were kidnapped – we want to know how you got away."

"It was down to Tom. He's my hero."

Anne and Tom looked into each other's eyes and I could see that true love had not only taken root, but had grown into a sturdy shoot and was beginning to produce twigs and flowers to boot.

"Anne will have to tell you about her ordeal and how it ended another time, I'm afraid," Tom said, draining his cocoa. "There's no time to lose – I've got an urgent lead to follow, with a trail of clues that leads abroad, all the way to Australia. My boss in the police force wants me to get to the airport for a flight very early tomorrow. Goodbye, my darling Anne. You'll be safe now, back at St Hilda's."

Tom flung his arms round her and gave her an enormous kiss on her lips.

"Until we meet again!"

And with that, he was gone.

"So, tell us," Sister Phoebe demanded. "Tell us what happened."

Anne launched into a tale of skulduggery explaining how Cousin Philip's man had kidnapped her then held her captive in a remote farmhouse on the other side of Dorchester.

"Thank goodness I'd managed to leave that note for you, Trixie," she said. "However frightened I was, I knew that help would be on the way."

"Did you have any food?" I asked.

"It wasn't bad," she admitted, "especially compared to some of the stuff we have in the convent."

Sister Phoebe stifled a giggle before urging her to continue.

"Were you tied up?" I asked.

"No," Anne said. "I was locked in a room, but totally unharmed. They even brought me these fresh clothes to wear."

"Thank the Lord," Sister Phoebe whispered. "There have been times when I wondered..."

"Sister Phoebe wondered whether you might be as unlucky as Tess of the d'Urbervilles," I said.

"Oh no! Although when Philip arrived at the house, he immediately started on about my inheritance again and how it wasn't fair that my parents had been so wealthy when he had nothing."

"And was he still trying to persuade or force you to marry him before you reach 21 and can dispose of the money as you choose?"

"Yes, indeed," Anne said. "If I had given in to his demands, I actually wonder if I would have lived to see my 21st birthday."

The three of us fell silent as we contemplated the enormity of what Anne had escaped from.

"So is Philip locked up now?" I asked.

"Thankfully, yes," Anne said. "Tom and the police found where I was somehow, part hunch, part luck Tom said, and they burst in all guns blazing..."

"Guns!" Sister Phoebe's eyes lit up.

"Well, maybe not actual guns," Anne said. "Just a turn of phrase, but it was very exciting."

"And then they all got carted off to jail?" I said.

"Yes!" Anne clapped her hands together. "Tom is so wonderful! I love him even more now, if that is possible."

"You'll not be wanting your habit back, then," Sister Phoebe said. "Sounds as if a different life is on the cards for you; never did think you were suited to the convent life."

"Well..." Anne blushed and looked down. "I think you're right and maybe my future will take a different path."

"You need to take a different path," Sister Edward yelled as she swung through the door, followed by Cath, Natalie and a gaggle of girls from the Cubicles.

"I'm so sorry, Trixie," Cath said. "When I got back to bed after seeing you leaving for the Laundry, Natalie asked me who I'd been talking to."

"I've got very good hearing," Natalie said with a smirk.

"I had to tell her what you were up to..." Cath looked down at the floor.

"And I had to tell Sister Edward," Natalie said.

"Yes, and it's a jolly good thing they did," Sister Edward said, "although it's not what you think, Trixie. We've had a call from the police, you see. Anne's wicked Cousin Philip has escaped from police custody."

"Oh no!" Anne's hand flew to her mouth and several girls burst into tears.

"The police suspect Philip could be on his way here right now," Sister Edward said, "because he might think that Tom would have brought you to St Hilda's to be safe with us. That's what I meant when I said you'd better take a different path. You need to get out of here!"

"I'm in charge now; thank you, Sister Edward," a firm voice said.

Sister Ignatius! How did she know we were all here?

"I heard the commotion when out on my evening stroll," Sister Ignatius said. "It seemed a good idea to check the grounds after the call from the police and I happened to bump into my nephew Tom, ahem, Father Tom, as he was rushing off to the airport not five minutes ago. I can guess the rest. Question is: what do we do next?"

Cath, Natalie, myself and all the girls started talking at once then, delighted our opinions had been asked and anxious to help out with any advice we could think off, garnered from watching crime dramas on television in the holidays.

"Silence!" Sister Ignatius roared. "When I asked what we are going to do next, the question was, of course, rhetorical."

Natalie started to speak, and Sister Ignatius silenced her with a roar of, "Look it up, girl! Next time you are near a dictionary."

Complete silence reigned then, save for the tiny mechanical sound of the whirling cogs of Sister Ignatius' brain, trying this way and that to find a solution.

"I know," she said at last. "Sister Phoebe and Trixie will take Anne to safety. In the Mini."

"When?" Sister Phoebe asked.

"Now," Sister Ignatius said. "I've some sandwiches here you are welcome to take to sustain you on the journey."

She produced a large lump wrapped in greaseproof paper from the folds of her habit. "I often find I'm a little peckish in the evenings and so carry these with me," she explained. "Your need is greater than mine, so please, take them."

"Where are we going?" Anne asked.

"There's a place," Sister Ignatius said, "down in Devon, a house Trixie knows – her aunt and uncle's. They're away at the moment, isn't that right, Trixie? I believe their home is fairly remote and you probably know where the spare key is kept, being a family member."

"How do you know all this?" I demanded. "Have you been reading my letters?"

"Of course not," Sister Ignatius said.

"That would be down to me." Reverend Mother glided into the room. "It's my painful, and often rather tedious duty to read all the correspondence that comes into St Hilda's and everything that leaves it. Then I share the contents with Sister Ignatius."

"How did you know we were here?" I asked.

"I happened to be passing on my evening walk..."

I sighed. Everyone always said our letters weren't private, but I had hoped so much this wasn't true. Another illusion shattered.

"Yes," I said, "my aunt and uncle are away as it happens and yes, I do know where they keep the spare key."

"How long will it take us to get to Devon?" Sister Phoebe asked. "Where is Devon?"

Sister Ignatius shrugged her shoulders and looked at Sister Edward. Sister Edward looked blank and looked at Reverend Mother, who pronounced that it was probably quite a long way and might take a great deal of time, so we needed to get ready as quickly as we could, before any unwelcome visitors turned up.

The nuns might have only had a hazy idea of where Devon was, but their powers of organisation were phenomenal. Very soon a human chain had been dragooned into action and quantities of supplies for our trip were being ferried to the nuns' Mini, including clothes, toiletries, a map (actually it was an old school atlas, but we hoped it would do the job), and a bag of basic food provisions as we had no idea how long we would be away.

Sister Phoebe started up the motor.

"You forgot this! Here, Trixie, you take it." Natalie pushed the string bag bulging with biscuits into my eager hands through the open back window.

"Thank you, Natalie," I said.

"Sorry for being horrid," she muttered as the car jerked forward and stalled.

"No problem," I said. "I hadn't even noticed."

"And I have something for you, Trixie," Sister Edward said. "I was, of course, correct to take this from you but I think under the circumstances, as you are going away and may need something to occupy your time while in the car...well, here it is..."

She gave me a paper bag folded at the top. "Don't open this until you are out of Sister Ignatius' sight," she whispered.

I took the heavy bag and popped it on the floor by my feet, then almost immediately we were racing down the drive at full pelt; Sister Phoebe drove as if possessed and Anne sat in the front alongside her, clinging on to the door handle even more desperately than I had on my way to the optician that very morning.

"Oh, my glasses!" I said. "I won't be able to collect them next week."

"Sure we'll be back by next week," Sister Phoebe said. "Just you wait and see; it'll all be fine."

She swung round a bend in the road and we were dazzled by the headlights of an oncoming car.

Anne shrieked, "Oh no! Philip!" in terror as she recognised her tormentor in the car speeding towards us. I caught a glimpse of a nasty sneering face illuminated in the Mini's headlights; there was a disconcerting metallic clash of gears before Sister Phoebe continued racing down the drive, transporting us away from danger.

"Which way should I turn, Trixie?" she asked as we reached the end of the drive.

"Turn right," I said, taking a wild guess. "I'm sure it's right for Devon!"

Chapter 16

An epic journey

It was in our favour that Philip had no idea where we were headed; it was also in our favour that Sister Phoebe drove faster than anyone I have ever been given a lift by, either before or since this legendary occasion. Red lights were nothing to her, nor did she seem to have heard of giving way at junctions. I seriously began to wonder whether her foot would go through the floor of the car at one point, so determinedly did she press the accelerator pedal.

I squinted at the ink-stained school atlas in the back of the car with the aid of my pocket torch while Anne looked out for road signs to guide us on our way down to my aunt and uncle's home.

"At least we've managed to escape Philip," I said, turning to look out of the back window. "No sign of him following us."

"Don't be too sure," Anne said. "He's very cunning and might have taken a short cut and be waiting ahead."

"Stuff and nonsense," Sister Phoebe said. "Where's your sense of optimism? He's no match for me! If I hadn't become a nun, I was seriously thinking about a career in Formula One. Pass me a biscuit, Trixie dear – I could murder a squashed fly."

I passed the crumbly biscuit forward and offered one to Anne too. Sister Phoebe took a fierce bite as she swung round a sharp corner, causing a flurry of crumbs to spray into the back of the car. As I brushed my skirt clean, I happened to look down at my feet and saw the mysterious package Sister Edward had handed me as we had set off from St Hilda's. With eager fingers, I reached inside the bag and pulled out – *War and Peace*. I suppose this was the nearest a nun could get to saying sorry.

I lost myself in nineteenth century Russia using my torch again and so it was a while before I realised we were being tailed.

"Faster, Sister Phoebe," I urged. "Faster! There's a car right behind us and it's flashing its lights."

"OK," she said. "Turbo boost on..."

"Think you'd better stop," Anne said. "The car behind is a police car."

Sister Phoebe pulled over at once and greeted the officer with a winsome smile.

"Good evening, Madam," he said. "I've had a disturbing report of a car being driven without a driver, and what's more, being driven far too fast. I had assumed it would be a child joyriding, but it looks as if I was mistaken."

Sister Phoebe launched into a quick explanation

of why we were hurrying down to Devon as fast as we could.

"So you see, Officer," she concluded, "it really is a matter of life or death, which surely excuses the odd bit of speeding, and of course I can't help being rather small, can I? The Good Lord made me short of stature."

"But big of heart," Anne added.

The officer wrinkled his nose.

"Well," he said at last, "I can't see any real harm has been done, and if you promise to cut your speed and take all due care on the road, I think I can let you go on your way."

"Bless you, Officer," Sister Phoebe said, making the sign of the cross.

"You might want to move that rosary out of the way, though," the officer advised. "It is obscuring your vision a little, hanging over the driver's mirror like that. Not entirely safe, is it?"

"But Officer," Sister Phoebe cried, "surely it's safer to travel *with* rosary beads than without?"

The policeman scratched his chin. "Well, maybe..."

"Biscuit, Officer?" Sister Phoebe proffered a cellophane packet of her favourites. "You can keep the pack, if you like."

"Thank you kindly, Madam. Don't mind if I do. It can get peckish working these long night shifts."

"Heavens!" Anne shrieked, looking in the rear-view mirror. "It's Philip!"

I looked back and saw in the distance the bright

lights of a car hurtling towards us.

"Quick, Officer," Sister Phoebe said. "Not a moment to lose. You must let us drive off, then park your car across the road and arrest that man."

"Of course!"

The gallant officer sprang into action. My last view out of the back window was of him clutching the biscuits, smiling and waving, then shooting into his car and quickly moving it across the narrow lane to block Philip's way. We could hear loud hooting from a car horn as we sped away.

"Phew! That was close," Sister Phoebe said. "Better put my foot down."

"Yes," Anne agreed. "The officer might have given us a bit of time to get away, but Philip won't allow himself to be arrested."

"At least he doesn't know where we're going," I said.

"Yes, that's good," Anne replied. "He obviously knows we're travelling west, but won't know our exact destination."

Despite the drama, I must have fallen asleep soon after that because the next thing I remember is the car slowing down.

"Are we there yet?" I asked drowsily.

"Not quite, my dear," Sister Phoebe said. "We're at a petrol station."

I looked out of the side window to see an attendant filling the car. As the sickly smell of petrol filled my nostrils, I also noticed it was morning.

"How long have I been asleep?"

"Hours," Anne said. "You must have been shattered, poor thing."

"Time for Sister Ignatius' sandwiches, I think," Sister Phoebe said as we sped off again.

Never have I been so grateful for a sandwich as on this occasion. The slightly soggy cheese and tomato creation made with margarine and Mother's Shame processed bread had undoubtedly been far too long in Sister Ignatius' pocket before she'd generously presented it to us as we set off on our journey, and its condition probably hadn't been helped by being squished by vast quantities of Sister Phoebe's biscuits – but to me, it tasted like nectar. I sank my teeth into the savoury softness and settled back in my seat to admire the early morning light as we passed through some of the most glorious countryside in England.

"When we get near, Trixie," Anne said, "I'll be relying on you to help with directions to your aunt and uncle's house."

"Mgwah," I mumbled, my mouth full of food. I screwed up my eyes, trying to remember the last time I'd been to their house.

It had been Christmas last year, before my parents' move to Italy had even been dreamt about. We'd spent a very happy week there over the festive period before driving back home for the New Year. All of a sudden, my eyelids prickled. My parents! I tried really hard not to think about them generally, but I did miss them. This wouldn't do; I pulled myself together. At least my parents were still alive, not like poor Anne's. Fancy losing your parents at the age of eighteen, like she had...

"She's nodding off again," I heard Anne saying just before I slipped away, the rhythm of the car gently lulling me into another world.

Chapter 17

Arrival at Seaway House

"Trixie! Trixie!" Anne's gentle face appeared in front of me as I woke to find we had stopped by the side of the road looking over the sparkling sea. Stretching, I rubbed my eyes.

"We need your help now," she said. "We know we must be near *Seaway House*, but..."

"It's just round the corner," I said. "We're only seconds away – I can't believe it!"

I opened the car door, intending to get out and take a proper look at the familiar sea view, but Anne had words of caution.

"Best not, Trixie," she advised. "We don't know if we're still being followed."

"Very unlikely," Sister Phoebe said. "We can get out and take a look, surely?"

Anne frowned. "You don't know Philip like I do. He might not be following us, but he has a team of criminals who work for him and they stretch all over the country – actually, I suspect it's all over the world. He's a real piece of work."

I shut the car door and Sister Phoebe started the engine again.

"Turn right here," I advised. "Yes, this is the lane, that's it. Now, keep going and it's the first house on the right – the only house on the right."

I was comforted to see the familiar painted sign of *Seaway House*.

Anne hopped out and opened the wooden gate, and Sister Phoebe drove over the crunchy shingle.

"The garage is round to the left," I said. "You could park in front of it."

"We should park inside it," Sister Phoebe said, "if we can. Less obvious that someone's here. Do you think it's locked?"

Anne tried the door. "Yes!"

"I know where my aunt keeps the house keys; maybe the garage key is with them?" I suggested.

I ran round to the front of the house, to the main door which faced the large garden and looked out over the sea. Multiple pots of geraniums stood all along the terrace, still with many fine blooms.

"One, two, three..." I counted. The keys were always under the seventh pot; ah, success. I flew back to the garage where Anne and Sister Phoebe were waiting.

"I think this might be the one," I said, trying a small Yale key.

"Brilliant, Trixie!" Sister Phoebe said as the door swung open. "I'll just drive the car in..."

We crept in through the back door, thought I am not sure what we expected to find as we already knew there was no one at home.

"What a lovely house," Anne exclaimed. "So

cosy."

"And such a great view," Sister Phoebe said as she wandered over to the front of the kitchen to look out at the same view of the sparkling sea we had seen from the road below. "An amazing hide-away."

"Just the job!" Anne said. "Now, I'll take these bags upstairs, then we need to think about what we're going to have to eat. It's been a long time since those sandwiches."

"My aunt always has plenty of stores," I said, flinging open the door to the pantry. It was full of rows of home-made preserves, bags of rice, jars of flour, and various tinned goods.

"And we've got the food Reverend Mother gave us from the convent kitchen too," Sister Phoebe said, "although I like the look of what's in this pantry much better."

I knew what she meant. I'd already looked in the bag from Reverend Mother and it was mostly stuffed with processed bread, industrial quantities of margarine and the sort of jam that doesn't have any fruit in.

"I know how to get the stove going," I said. "Once that's on, the house will warm up and we can boil a kettle and make tea."

Sister Phoebe flopped into a chair.

"I don't mind admitting I feel a little tired. It was a long drive through the night..."

"She's already asleep," Anne whispered to me, seconds later. "Must be exhausted. At least you and

I managed to get some rest on the journey down here. Such a shame I never learnt to drive."

I fetched a blanket from upstairs and laid it over Sister Phoebe's tiny frame, then set about making tea while Anne paced up and down.

"I won't feel secure until I know Philip is behind bars again," she said. "Oh, I do wish Tom was here, or I had some way of getting in contact with him."

"What's he doing in Australia?" I asked. "He didn't really say why he had to go there in such a hurry."

"No," Anne said. "He said he couldn't tell me, thought it wasn't right to get my hopes up or something, but they'd had unverified reports of a really big crime they thought Philip had committed out there and it was imperative they sent a team out to investigate. If there is any news, he'll telephone Sister Ignatius. We should do the same in a while, to let her know we've arrived safely."

"Good idea." I plonked the teapot down on the table. "I'll see if there are any biscuits left."

Anne sighed. "Don't suppose there might be anything apart from biscuits? I rather feel as if I've had carbohydrate overload on the way down here."

I grinned. "I'm sure you don't want anything from the convent bag of food, especially the bread, but I know how to make bread from the flour in my aunt's pantry. I could get started on that and later, perhaps we could have sardines on toast, but if you want something instant, for now the choice is probably tinned fruit or biscuits."

Anne laughed. "Biscuits," she decided. "But maybe something other than the wretched squashed fly ones? You can have too much of a good thing...and maybe some tinned fruit as well?"

After tea, tinned mandarins, some cheese biscuits and custard creams, Anne said she would ring the convent.

"Do you think I should ring your aunt and uncle to say we're here, as well? We seem to have decided to stay here without permission and it would be good to have their blessing."

"I don't have a number for them," I said. "I'm sure they mentioned the name of their hotel in the Lake District, but I can't quite remember. The Lakeside View? Lake View? Something like that?"

"Not to worry," Anne said. "No point in trying to ring your parents, I suppose?"

"I don't know their number," I said, "because I'm not allowed to ring abroad, but Sister Ignatius probably has a way of getting in contact with them for emergencies. You could try asking her when you speak on the phone."

"OK," Anne said.

I washed up everything from our snack while aware of Anne's gentle voice from the hall. She must be speaking to Sister Ignatius now. I stoked up the fire and then snuggled up in a rocking chair next to Sister Phoebe who was still asleep.

Suddenly I wished I was lying in my bed in the Cubicles reading under the bedclothes with a torch. Normal life, however constricting, seemed very attractive compared to this strange and rather frightening situation we now found ourselves in.

Sister Phoebe stirred beside me then woke up.

"Don't look so worried," she said. "I've got my rosary beads and we've got right on our side. We need to keep calm."

Anne came back into the room.

"Everything OK?" I asked.

"Yes, I think so."

"You think so? What did they say?" Sister Phoebe asked.

"It's not what they said," Sister Anne continued. "The nuns were all very pleased to hear of our safe arrival and I've asked Sister Ignatius to contact your parents and they will contact your aunt and uncle to let them know we're here – that's all fine."

"What is it, then?" Sister Phoebe said.

"It might be nothing, but when I was on the phone telling Sister Ignatius we'd arrived safely at *Seaway House*, I distinctly heard a clicking sound on the telephone line."

"A clicking sound?" Sister Phoebe sat up in her chair and knitted her fingers together. "A clicking sound? Oh, drat and double drat!"

"What does it mean?" Anne asked.

Sister Phoebe scowled. "It means that someone's been listening in to your conversation, that's what a click on the line means."

"Really?" Anne said. "How do you know?"

"Saw it in a film, one of those spy thrillers," Sister Phoebe said. "I was supervising the Sixth Form in the gym one Sunday afternoon. We had hired a film that seemed a little scary, with lots of creeping about and guns – it was about the Cold War. Rather unsuitable, so in the end Sister Edward pulled the plug out of the projector which was a shame because we never got to see the end of it…"

"Sister Phoebe!" Anne's voice became shrill. "Please! Stick to the point. Do you think my conversation with Sister Ignatius could have been overheard?"

"Yes, I do!" Sister Phoebe sprang up and adjusted the cape of her habit, like the super hero that she was. "Triple drat," she shouted. "We're not safe here!"

Chapter 18

Danger!

I was so shocked I simply didn't know what to say or do for a few moments. The situation must be quite desperate if Sister Phoebe, a Woman of God, was uttering words such as 'drat'. And not just drat, but double drat, triple drat even.

Anne's face creased with concern. "Perhaps we should ring the police? Oh, I'm so sorry to cause all this bother. This whole situation is because of me. If my parents hadn't left me so much money, then Philip wouldn't be pursuing me in this ridiculous fashion, trying to get his hands on my fortune..."

"And his hands on you," Sister Phoebe said. "Don't forget he wants to marry you. As if that's going to happen..."

Her next words were drowned by a thunderous roar from the garden. Heavy rain was lashing at the windows of *Seaway House* and a bitter groaning sound was coming from the old hawthorn tree in the garden. A sudden autumn storm was in full swing. Peering out of the window, I watched the hawthorn split and fall, the scene illuminated by jagged forks and ear-splitting claps. Sister Phoebe and Anne joined me and we all three stood in a terrified row, looking out at the dismal and dramatic scene.

"I think there's someone out there," Anne whispered. "Just there, see, by the front door?"

I looked out but it was quite dark and difficult to make out. Perhaps there was a shape moving around, perhaps not...

"We definitely need to ring the police," Anne said. "Now!"

Sister Phoebe rushed to the hall and snatched up the receiver. "Oh no! The line's dead. Must be the storm."

"Trixie!" Anne said. "Where's the nearest neighbour?"

"There aren't any immediate neighbours," I said. "That's why my aunt and uncle chose the house – they love the solitude. We'll have to go into the village if we want to find another phone."

"OK, but I'm going alone," Anne said. "You two are safer here. Lock the door behind me and don't open it for anyone – promise?"

"Not even you?" Sister Phoebe asked.

"Of course, for me," Anne said. "You know what I mean. Don't open the door for anyone apart from me."

The light had completely faded now and the storm had retreated, just a few hisses and crackles as the night settled.

Anne donned a raincoat and wellington boots we found by the backdoor and got ready to leave.

"Wait," I said as she was about to step out. "Shouldn't we come with you? Philip probably knows where we are now and…"

"Yes," Sister Phoebe said, "and if he's the mastermind of a vast criminal empire – I've seen that in a film too – then he might even now be on his way here or be sending someone local to finish you off. We need to protect you, Anne – you're not safe going out on your own."

Anne sighed. "I suppose you could be right and maybe we shouldn't be taking any chances by not sticking together."

Within a few seconds, Sister Phoebe and I were dressed in over-sized raincoats ready for our great adventure.

"Shall I bring some biscuits?" Sister Phoebe asked, finding her string bag. "I could restock, if you're sure your aunt won't mind, Trixie."

"Leave it," Anne said. "No time for snacks."

I let out a long sad sigh.

"Oh, all right then," Anne said. "Maybe one or two packets, but not more than that."

As we made our way towards the garage, there was the unmistakable sound of a car slowly approaching down the lane. As I was the smallest and least noticeable, I ran to the gate to see what was going on. The car was cruising towards *Seaway House* with only its side lights on.

I sneaked back to the garage. "If we get the car out, whoever it is will hear us," I whispered.

"Let's wait and see if the car stops here," Anne

said. "It may be nothing to do with us or with Philip."

We shrank back against the hedge at the side of the garage and held our breaths. The car stopped right outside *Seaway House* and all three of us concealed ourselves, creeping down the side of the garage against the prickly shrubs.

We heard the gate slowly opening, then two burly men began to make their way across the shingle, through the garden and round to the front door on the far side of the house. I knew it was madness but I couldn't help following them.

"Why did we have to come out in this weather?" one man hissed.

"I've already told you," the other snarled. "The phone lines are down, otherwise we could've rung the women to threaten them; now we have to do it in person."

"Who are we doing this job for anyway?" the first man asked.

"It's that Philip bloke, you know him; he's over from Australia at the moment. Got some mad scheme concerning a young woman I believe."

"Mmm, shame – I was just getting cosy with the missus in front of the fire with a Lancashire hotpot. Still, have to take the work where you can these days." "And you daren't say no to Philip."

"So, exactly what is it we have to do, then?"

"Bit of threatening, bit of fist waving, nothing drastic. Then report back."

"And where's Philip now?"

"He's waiting in Dartmouth, at some fancy hotel. Driven all the way down from Dorset apparently; doesn't like to do his own dirty work, you know that."

My knees were wobbling at the thought of nearly meeting these two ruffians; it looked as though we'd got out of the house in the nick of time.

I ran back to Anne and Sister Phoebe. "Quick! We need to drive away. The men are round at the front door but they'll soon realise we're not there and start looking for us."

"Got the key to the garage?" Sister Phoebe asked.

"No, I thought you still had it," Anne said.

"I haven't got it either," I said. "I think it's on the kitchen table – that's the last place I saw it. Oh, what are we going to do?"

"We're going to make our way to the village on foot," Sister Phoebe said. "Do you know the way, Trixie?"

"I know how to get there over the fields, a short cut," I said. "I've got my pocket torch with me too; I always carry it in case I get the chance to read."

The three of us fled through the gate, across the lane and into the field opposite, melting into the hedgerows, following an overgrown foot path I'd known for years but which hopefully would be unfamiliar to the men trying to frighten us.

As we slipped away, we heard a bellow of rage.

"They're not here! Must have legged it. We'll be for it now with the boss."

Chapter 19

Police to the rescue

The storm was no more than a memory as we made our way across the fields, helped by my pocket torch and the light of the moon.

"If we weren't running away from a couple of ruffians sent by a criminal mastermind, this would be a very pleasant evening," Sister Phoebe remarked.

"Keep your voice down," Anne urged. "You don't know how close the men are now."

"Indeed!" Sister Phoebe whispered. "Sorry!"

"What's that rattling sound?" I asked a little while later.

"Apologies!" Sister Phoebe said. "Just my rosary beads."

We soon reached the village and fell upon the welcome red telephone box with joy, getting through to the police in seconds and being collected by a policeman in his car within minutes.

"We really appreciate this, Officer," Sister Phoebe said. "Would you like a Garibaldi biscuit?"

The policeman guffawed. "My mate who works in traffic, up in Dorset, he said you'd offered him biscuits; he said you were quite a character."

Sister Phoebe beamed to hear this. "He was wonderful," she said. "He held back the monstrous Philip by parking his car across the road. That was my idea you know – although to be honest, I..."

"Saw it in a film?" I finished for her and we all laughed.

"It did the trick," the policeman said, "at least it held this Philip character back for a while, long enough to let you make off."

"What happened next?" I asked.

"Well, in the end Philip reversed his car and shot off down another road," the policeman explained, "and my mate couldn't catch up with him. He called it in though and it was added to the long catalogue of misdemeanours committed by this rogue." The policeman gave a sudden bark of laughter. "Once we get him behind bars, he won't be coming out in a hurry."

Anne shuffled in her seat. "I know you think it's all a bit of a joke," she said, "but I've always felt Philip would be capable of something really bad one day. Horrifically bad."

"What sort of thing?" I asked.

"I don't really know," Anne answered. "It's just a feeling I have, an instinct, if you like; I think he's quite ruthless."

"Just as well we're on his tail," the policeman said, in a more sober voice this time. "Don't you worry, love; we'll soon have him banged to rights. He can't get away."

"The men said he was staying in a hotel in Dartmouth," I offered.

"Why didn't you tell me that straight away?" The policeman snatched up his car radio.

"Here, Sarge, you know that Philip you're looking for – he's apparently holed up in a hotel in Dartmouth. Which one? Don't rightly..."

"It's the *Smugglers' Den*," I said.

"Hear that Sarge? Need to send someone there now, to the *Smugglers' Den*."

I folded my hands in my lap with satisfaction; at last, I'd been useful. Eavesdropping was supposed to be wrong, a sin, but it had proved very useful on this occasion.

"What do you mean it's after hours and you don't have anyone else who can get there quickly?" the policeman yelled. "That's not good enough! I've got a schoolgirl, a young lady and a nun in the back of my patrol car and they need to know this criminal's being dealt with."

"We could go!" Leaning forward, I repeated my suggestion in an even louder voice in case the policeman on the other end of the radio hadn't quite heard. "We could go and capture Philip. I know the way to the hotel – I've been there for tea with my aunt and uncle – it's not far from here and it would be so much fun."

"Oh, yes please!" Sister Phoebe squealed. "It would be just like that part of the adventure film I saw with the Upper Five last winter, the one where..."

"Silence!" the policeman roared. "I can't hear what the Sarge is saying. OK, yes, we'll be very, very careful...yes, at no time will they be in any danger...yes, and I'll report back as soon as...and you'll telephone the hotel and ask the manager to keep an eye on Philip, to make sure he stays put..."

The policeman replaced the radio and turned round.

"Looks like we're on, ladies! Stay behind me at all times; you're going to be witnessing an arrest."

As the patrol car drew near to the *Smugglers' Den*, the policeman said,

"You know I was exaggerating, ladies; I can't let you take any risks, so you won't actually be witnessing me arrest Philip – I'll be leaving you safely in the reception where the manager will look after you, while I go upstairs and capture this idiot who's been such a nuisance to everyone all over the country."

Sister Phoebe and I slumped back in our seats as we heard this. It was so disappointing. I'd never seen anyone be arrested before and I expect Sister Phoebe hadn't, in fact I felt sure of it.

"Look!" Anne screamed. "Over there – it's Philip!"

"Where?" the policeman said. "You mean he's not in the hotel?"

"Definitely not," Anne said. "I've just spotted him walking past that sign over there, the one pointing to the harbour; he's wearing a hat pulled right down over his eyes, but he doesn't fool me."

We followed in the car, closely but cautiously, until the road ended and turned into a narrow pedestrian-only lane. Abandoning his car, the policeman jumped out, hand ready on his truncheon.

"You three stay in the car, d'you hear?"

"Of course, Officer," Sister Phoebe said as she raced after him. "You can trust me implicitly. I am a woman of God."

Under her breath, she muttered, "And we all know God helps those who help themselves."

My heart was racing as I pursued her; I'd have such tales to tell in the Cubicles! Surely this would guarantee my popularity for ever afterwards with Natalie and her coven?

Philip must have realised he was being followed because he broke into a run

and we all charged down the alley towards the sea. Very soon the burly policeman had grabbed Philip by the scruff of his neck and pinned him against the rough stone wall of a house. What a hero!

"Couldn't be bothered to go and frighten these ladies from what we've heard," the policeman said. "Sent some of your men over to *Seaway House* to terrify them."

"Anne!" Philip shouted. "Forgive me! I meant no harm. It's just that I..."

"Save it!" Sister Phoebe yelled. "We all know you're only after her money. Don't pretend you're in love with her. We won't believe you."

Philip struggled a bit but then gave himself up, holding his hands out willingly for the handcuffs.

"Coward through and through," Sister Phoebe pronounced.

"I'm not so sure," Anne said. "I still think he's hiding something, something much worse..."

"Ha!" Philip barked. "Of course, dear Anne, your instincts are correct. There's something much, much worse, but you'll never find out what it is. I'll take that secret to my grave."

"What is it?" Anne demanded. "You have to tell us."

"No way! I'm not telling you that – it would spoil the fun. You'll never find out what I've done. What I've buried."

Chapter 20

Return to St Hilda's

Once we were finally back at school at the end of the week, it took about ten minutes before the entire community of girls and nuns knew every single detail of all our goings on during our trip to Devon, down to exactly how many biscuits we had all consumed and what a wicked man Philip was. Speculation was rife about when Tom would return and marry Anne, which we hoped would be very soon.

And I had been right – my trip did make a difference with Natalie and her cronies; they treated me with a new respect and I was invited to join in games of jacks, dance Scottish reels and hare round the corridors at top speed with quantities of new friends on a daily basis.

My parents phoned me from abroad, which was an almost unheard-of extravagance; when I took the call in the tiny telephone room, I was ecstatic to hear their familiar voices and told them all about my adventures. They even offered to come back to England at once if I needed them to, but while I was touched by their concern, I assured them it wasn't necessary. I felt a warm glow though, to think they would do that for me.

There were at least fifty girls listening outside the door of the tiny phone room while I talked to my parents; usually the queue was about ten girls long but news of the international call had spread like wildfire, resulting in an unruly scrum. It seemed everyone wanted to be able to say that they had been queuing for the phone when a call from Rome was in progress.

I had a lovely postcard from the Lake District from my aunt and uncle; they didn't seem to mind at all that we'd taken shelter in their house and said they were very much looking forward to my visit at half term, which was really quite soon now, just a month away.

Anne stayed in the convent for the time being, because she didn't know quite what else to do. Although she had definitely decided she didn't have a vocation to become a nun, she also didn't want to go home to her country estate alone while Tom was still in Australia. The police thought it for the best too, if Anne were to stay on protected by the safety of the convent until Tom returned.

Very soon, Anne was offered a job as a drama teacher at St Hilda's for as long as she wanted, which suited everyone, especially us girls. We'd never had a teacher who was so much fun.

As for Philip, he was, in the immortal words of the policeman we had met in Devon, 'banged to rights, good and proper.'

"Do you think he will be sentenced to hard labour?" Sister Phoebe asked me one evening when I was visiting her in the Laundry with Cath.

"Have you been watching old films again, Sister Phoebe?" Cath asked.

"Hm," I said. "I don't think anyone does hard labour any more – at least, not in the UK."

Sister Phoebe's face fell to hear this.

"Surely you believe in forgiveness, Sister," I asked. "Perhaps Philip is sorry for what he did, for kidnapping Anne?"

"Yes," Cath said, "and planning to steal all her money."

"You're right." Sister Phoebe bowed her head. "We should be generous towards criminals. I know that's right."

"What's that you're saying about criminals?"

I turned and saw Anne coming into the Laundry, looking a little downcast.

"What's wrong?" I asked.

"Nothing much," she said. "It's just that I miss Tom so much. He's taking a long time to get back from Australia."

"Keep the faith," Sister Phoebe advised. "Your man is a good one, that's for sure, and I know you'll be together in the end."

"I'm worried about what Philip said," Anne mumbled, tears falling freely now. "He said we'd never know what secrets he'd buried. I can't get a terrible thought out of my head – what if, what if..."

"There, there." Sister Phoebe walked over to Anne and took her hand. "Don't you fret – it'll all be fine. I'm sure he didn't mean what you think he meant. He was probably just trying to wind everyone up..."

"Do you mean, what if he killed your parents?" I asked.

"Trixie!" Cath put her hand to her mouth. "You can't go around saying things like that with no evidence...it's, it's not right."

Sister Phoebe reprimanded me with a glare, but I felt I was only saying what the others had thought. We had never really discussed that horribly dramatic time when Philip had been cornered in the alley down by the harbour in Dartmouth and had poured out his venomous words, words that had sent a chill down my spine, and no doubt Anne's too.

"I, I have sometimes wondered if he killed my parents," Anne admitted. "But how would he have got away with it? It seems preposterous that he might have somehow staged a car accident and murdered them."

"How did he seem at their funeral?" I asked.

"He was very calm; he took charge and arranged everything which was what I wanted because I was in bits at the time. I was too young, not ready for such a tragedy."

"No one's ever ready," Sister Phoebe muttered.

"I refuse to feel sorry for myself," Anne said, wiping her tears away. "Lots of people lose their parents."

The rest of us said nothing, but I know Cath and Sister Phoebe were thinking the same thing, how sad it was for Anne to have lost her parents at the age of eighteen when she had no siblings or other family save the dreadful Philip. All the money she was due to inherit when she turned 21 was no substitute for her loss; it meant nothing and I know she would have given it up in a trice if somehow she could have had her parents restored to her.

"I know how to cheer you up," I offered. "Why don't you teach us how to do your famous limp? Then we could get everyone to limp into Assembly one day? It would be such fun."

"Great idea, Trixie!" Anne stood up, then stooped forward with a groan and staggered about clutching her side and moaning. Cath and I practised and practised across the floor of the Laundry, with the smell of washing powder and starch billowing about us and the heat of the driers warming us, until we were laughing so much we couldn't continue.

Then Sister Phoebe joined in, hobbling and limping, wheezing and generally messing about.

The door suddenly flew open. "Sister Phoebe! What are you doing?"

Sister Edward stood resplendent with her black conduct book ready. "You girls should be in the Cubicles by now, so two conduct marks each. You look untidy too, Trixie, so take an extra conduct mark."

"Shouldn't that be an order mark? For untidiness?" I asked. "Conduct marks are for how you behave and order marks are for keeping things like possessions and your appearance in order."

"Quite right," Sister Edward boomed. "Thank you, Trixie. Take an order mark as well."

"Is that order mark as well as the three conduct marks, or are you reducing the conduct marks to two and adding one order mark?" I enquired.

"Cheeky girl!" Sister Edward yelled. "Take another order mark, oh, I mean a conduct mark – now you're getting me in a muddle."

Cath and I ran off laughing heartily before Sister Edward could punish us anymore.

Once back at the Cubicles, I found twenty girls crammed into my tiny cell, anxious to hear the latest gossip about Anne, but I didn't say a word about how she had broken down in the Laundry, considering that a private matter; I merely contented myself with demonstrating the limp that we were all to try out in Assembly the next morning.

Chapter 21

Nearly Christmas

Time flew past, and still Tom didn't return from Australia. Half-term came and went – spent in *Seaway House* with my aunt and uncle as planned – and the weeks started whizzing by to Christmas with all the usual excitement and high spirits.

One Sunday morning we were sitting in our classroom after Chapel, wearing full school uniform as we did from one end of the term to the other, waiting to hear what we were allowed to say in our weekly letters home. This would be our last letter writing session before the Christmas holidays. Those of us who lived abroad would probably arrive home before the letters reached our parents, but that was not thought to be a good enough reason to cancel the activity.

Sister Edward pointed to the board where she had written 'The News' and underlined it twice.

"This is your news," she said. "You have had a lovely time as always, you have had delicious meals..."

Here she had to break off to glare at Natalie who had gone cross-eyed and was shaking her head violently while we all sniggered.

"Take a conduct mark, Natalie, for insubordination…as I was saying, you may mention the charming film you were permitted to watch last Sunday afternoon in the gym and you may mention the uplifting sermon from Father Cuthbert in this morning's service."

Sighing, I unzipped my tan leather writing case, extracted a sheet of Basildon Bond and picked up my italic fountain pen. I toyed with the idea of ignoring the list on the board and writing whatever I wanted to my parents but had found from bitter experience that it wasn't worth it as you would find your letter quickly returned to you if you did that. Besides, there really was very little news to tell, now all the drama of the first few weeks of term had quietened down.

Then a very strange thing happened.

Sister Ignatius popped her head round the door and beckoned Sister Edward towards her urgently. As soon as both nuns had left the room, we all threw down our pens and ran to peer through the glass window in the door, desperate to find out what was going on.

"Ouch, you're stepping on my toes."

"Stop pulling my hair."

"Who's at the front? Can you tell us what's happening?"

"Nothing's happening," I whispered back. "They're just talking and if you pipe down we might have some chance of listening to their conversation."

"You're telling me that both of them..." Sister Edward was saying.

"Yes, both; isn't it amazing?" Sister Ignatius replied.

"What an evil person."

"And the police know, of course."

"Is Tom back now?"

"Yes! I haven't told Anne yet, though; he asked me not to..."

Suddenly Sister Edward noticed the window of the classroom door was completely full of eager faces and she clapped her hands to indicate we should sit down.

A few minutes later, she came into the room to find us practising our limping and wasn't even remotely cross. Something was afoot. So to speak.

"Girls!" She clapped her hands again. "May I have your attention? I have an announcement. You will be pleased to know that there really is a God and wonderful, marvellous things do happen and good people are rewarded."

I felt puzzled to hear this. What sort of an announcement was this, to be told there was a God? From a nun? As if it were news to her? All very curious.

The plot thickened when Sister Ignatius put her head round the door to say,

"Letter writing is cancelled for today – no letters will be sent because something much more exciting is happening and you are all to go the Hall and gather round the Christmas tree immediately, at the double."

She flounced away, leaving so quickly her veil streamed out horizontally behind her. Never had I seen a nun move at such a speed.

Within minutes, the entire school was crammed round the vast Christmas tree on a bright December morning, all agog.

Anne and the nuns sat on chairs and the girls found spaces on every square inch of the floor of the entrance Hall, all the way up the wide staircase, and on the bannisters.

Suddenly Tom appeared from the Ante Room. He strode over to the fireplace to stand next to the tree, his eyes bright and his face curved into the most wonderful smile. It took him about a micro second to locate Anne, and another micro second for a collective 'Ah' of joy to burst forth from the entire community, even including Sister Edward, and ripple around the vast Entrance Hall.

"Ladies," Tom said, "and Father Cuthbert too, of course," he added, indicating the priest sitting quietly and modestly at the back of the room. "I have returned from Australia and have such wonderful news."

"You're going to marry Anne!" a bold voice cried out.

"May we all be bridesmaids?" another voice yelled.

"Will you be married in the school Chapel?" a third shrieked.

"Ahem," Tom said, scarlet with embarrassment. "I, er, I haven't actually asked…"

"The answer would be yes," Anne said, "that is, if you were to ask me."

She stood up and the pair flew together in a warm embrace while everyone cheered. I took my glasses out of my pocket and popped them onto my nose so that I wouldn't miss any tiny detail of the beautifully romantic sight.

"But that's not all, my darling, darling Anne," Tom said. "You must have wondered why I have taken so long to come back to you and you must have wondered why I couldn't share the details of my investigation, but it had to stay completely hush-hush."

"I never doubted you for a minute," Anne said, gazing into her beloved Tom's eyes. "I love you forever."

"Look away, girls," Sister Edward advised. "Close your eyes!"

But it was too late. We were all swooning with the romanticism of Tom and Anne kissing in front of the whole school and forgetting that anyone else in the world existed.

"Tom!" Sister Ignatius reminded him. "Your other news, please."

"Ah, yes," he said, holding Anne's hand. "This will be a shock, dear Anne, but I have two people here who haven't seen you for a long time, not since they went on holiday when you were eighteen and didn't come back. Sister Phoebe – would be so kind?"

Sister Phoebe opened the front door to reveal a middle-aged couple with beaming smiles plastered on their faces, scanning the crowd to look for their daughter, Anne.

An amazing scene followed as Anne saw her parents again for the first time for many years and flung herself into their welcoming arms.

Sister Ignatius explained to us that Tom had been investigating Philip's big secret out in Australia all this time since the autumn; he and a team of police had cleverly discovered Philip's hidden crime – he had faked the car accident that had supposedly killed Anne's parents, leaving her a vulnerable heiress. The car crash had been cleverly staged, with Philip pretending to identify the nonexistent bodies, and the funeral had taken place with empty coffins.

"Philip is the head of a vast criminal empire," Sister Ignatius said, "which is how he managed to stay one step ahead of the police and evade justice for so long, carrying on with his skulduggery and behaving extremely reprehensibly."

So, Anne had been right when she had suspected that Philip's worst crime was yet to be uncovered.

"Philip was trying to get his hands on Anne's fortune," Sister Ignatius said. "She would have inherited a vast amount on her twenty first birthday, the 14th of December – tomorrow. Of course, now she will not inherit for what we all hope is a very, very long time because her parents have been found again. Has anyone any questions? Reverend Mother and I will do our best to answer them. Yes, Natalie?"

"Will Philip go to prison after his trial?"

"Yes indeed," Sister Ignatius said. "His crimes already known about justify a jail sentence but this latest shocking revelation means that he will be seeing the inside of a prison cell for quite some time to come, if not forever."

"Where have Anne's parents been all this time?" Cath asked.

"They were taken prisoner and kept out in the desert in Australia in a religious cult, which is a terrible thing to do to anyone," Reverend Mother explained. "They were treated humanely, and given plenty of food and exercise, but they weren't allowed to leave or make contact with people outside the cult. They were prisoners until Tom and his team discovered where they were and rescued them."

"Shocking!" Natalie called out, while I merely raised an eyebrow, thinking about how we were treated at school.

But then I realised that for some time a strange feeling had been sweeping over me, a feeling that I was actually beginning to enjoy being imprisoned at school. I supposed I was settling in at last, finding my feet, finding my friends, and finding a way to be myself in this strange World of Women – while still gathering an inordinate amount of conduct marks on a daily basis.

Sister Phoebe caught my eye then and started giggling, and before long the whole school was either giggling or crying hysterically, until in the end Sister Ignatius had to clap her hands and call for quiet.

"Remember you are young ladies," she begged, while struggling herself not to succumb to the myriad emotions flying around. "This sort of behaviour really won't do, will it?"

"I think we should sing a Christmas Carol," Reverend Mother suggested, "since we're all here round the tree together and we're in the run up to the end of term. Any preferences? Yes, Trixie – you've got your hand up."

"Joy to the World," I said, "because that's what we're all feeling isn't it?"

Everyone joined in, with Tom and Anne gazing into each other's eyes in a wonderfully soppy and romantic way, and Anne's parents standing one either side of her to make a daughter sandwich, hugging her as if they would never let her go.

Joy to the World...

About The Author

Jenny Worstall

Jenny is a writer and musician living in South London. You will find her playing the piano, singing in a choir or gossiping with her friends (essential research for her writing).

She is a member of the Romantic Novelists' Association and the Society of Women Writers and Journalists.

Her writing reflects her love of music and a tendency not to take life too seriously.

If you have enjoyed this book or any other book by Jenny Worstall, why not leave a review on Amazon? It's easy to do and doesn't have to be long – who knows, you might help another reader discover Jenny's books!

Printed in Great Britain
by Amazon